CAROLINA HURRICANE

CAROLINA HURRICANE

Shannon Dauphin

Black Lyon Publishing, LLC

Our books may be ordered through your local bookstore or by visiting the publisher:

www.BlackLyonPublishing.com

Black Lyon Publishing, LLC
PO Box 567
Baker City, OR 97814

This is a work of fiction. All of the characters, names, events, organizations and conversations in this novel are either the products of the author's vivid imagination or are used in a fictitious way for the purposes of this story.

ISBN-10: 1-934912-01-8
ISBN-13: 978-1-934912-01-0
Library of Congress Control Number: 2008921584

Published and printed in
the United States of America.

Black Lyon Contemporary Romance

For my husband,
who fills every day with romance.

Chapter One

Jordan dropped the stack of student essays into his briefcase and closed it. The locks on either side latched with twin snickers as he took a deep breath and looked around the classroom.

The desks were empty now, the students long gone. Most of the students at Sweetwater College didn't have classes on Friday—only the very dedicated or the very unlucky with scheduling wound up in Dr. Eversole's last class of the week, Advanced English Composition.

It might be a Friday afternoon, but Jordan's work wasn't done yet. He still had that stack of essays to grade, a test to create, and a lecture to prepare. He had a quiet house to go back to, just him and Callie the Cat. He might stop for dinner on the way out of town, something at that new restaurant over by the river. He had hoped to wait until he could take someone special out to eat with him, but the prospects were few and far between.

He looked out over the desks one more time before he turned out the light. It was a good class this time, filled with students who really wanted to learn. Those who didn't were outnumbered and as a result, even the slackers were seeing their grades rise. There were a few who had turned out to be outstanding writers, with the kind of raw talent a teacher always loves to see. He was sure more than a few of those essays in his briefcase would be stand-outs. He was always proud of his students, but this year was proving to be excellent, indeed.

Jordan made his way down the hallway. Everyone had already gone home for the weekend. The Frost Building was old, one of the first ones built on the campus, and the floors creaked with the satisfying sound of well-worn age. He paused to look around the commons area and saw nothing out of place.

The double doors of Frost opened onto a view of the enormous quad, a stunning twenty acres of healthy green grass and majestic trees. When the campus had been built in the late 1800s most of the trees had been carefully protected, so as to leave the place with its natural look and feel. As a result, the massive trees now towered over the weathered buildings like gentle guardians. There were usually dozens of students on the quad, taking advantage of the heavenly shade.

Around the side of the building was the parking lot. His convertible was parked right in his reserved spot, the space closest to his office door—years of faithful service to the college had its perks. The top of the car was open, the leather warm from the South Carolina sun. He dropped his briefcase into the back seat and looked around the lot, checking things out as he always did. It was a habit as natural as breathing.

Jordan recognized the Dean's car. There was Ms. Sullivan's car, the new teacher who taught advanced calculus. There was a car with a flat tire. In that car was a young woman, talking on a cell phone. Jordan watched for a moment and when she turned her head in his direction, he recognized her as one of his own students.

He headed in her direction, hoping he could help. The closer he got, the more he could hear. She was gesturing in the air and cursing like a sailor. Jordan tried to hide a grin.

The grin disappeared when he got close enough to see she was crying.

"Amanda?"

He was interrupting her phone call, but he didn't care. She looked up at him, startled, and clicked the phone closed. Tears ran down her face. Her long brown hair was tied back in a ponytail. She tried to smile at him and failed miserably.

"Hello, Dr. Eversole." Her voice was shaky. She wiped the tears from her face with her fingertips, making an even bigger mess. Jordan reached into his pocket and found a handkerchief, which he passed to her through the open window. She took it gratefully.

"This is old-fashioned," she said, even as she used it to clean her face.

"What's going on, Amanda?"

Her ponytail bounced as she shook her head. Her face was drawn and her lips were puffy from crying. Jordan was impressed that she didn't cower or blush. Instead, she met his eyes and held them.

"My mother and I are fighting," she said. "I moved out of the house a few weeks ago. Got a place of my own. I'm a junior in college, for crying out loud. I'm twenty-one years old. I can move out if I want to, right? I'm doing alright, but Mom doesn't like the fact I moved. She thinks it has to do with her, and it doesn't, but I don't know how to make her see that."

Amanda sniffled and looked out the windshield.

"I called to ask her for help with the tire, because I don't have a spare. And she—she said ..." Amanda stopped talking and looked down at the steering wheel.

"She said you were on your own and you should deal with it yourself?" Jordan asked.

She nodded.

"Do you have Triple-A? Does your insurance cover roadside assistance?"

She shook her head. "No. I already checked."

He thought for a moment. "You tried your mother—what about your father?"

"He passed away ten years ago. It's just me and mom."

Jordan chose his words carefully. "You know, if I had a flat tire and no spare, I would need help, too. You did the right thing by calling your mom first. That's what anybody would think, right? Call the family and ask for help that way."

Amanda looked back up at him.

"This thing with your Mom—I know it's a serious thing, and I won't make light of it. But I will tell you that it will blow over. In the meantime, let's talk about what to do about this tire, okay?"

Amanda smiled gratefully at him. She got out of the car just as her cell phone rang. She didn't make a move to answer it. Jordan considered telling her to pick it up, but he also knew it was her decision, and his job as an educator only went so far. Besides that, while Amanda might be student, but she was an adult who didn't need any input from someone else about how to live her life. It was one of those moments every teacher dreads, when he or she is torn between what might be right and what might not be.

Still, he had to try. Jordan looked pointedly at the phone. Amanda looked steadily back at him, not giving an inch. The look of defiance in her eyes said all he needed to know.

He walked to the back of her car. It was a Honda known for good gas mileage, obviously well-kept, with just enough wear to show that it wasn't purchased new. The tire was completely flat, and he wasn't sure there was hope of salvaging it. He studied the tire for a moment, then looked back at his own car. His spare wouldn't quite fit, but it would be more than suitable to get her to the nearest tire shop, and they could go from there.

"We'll take care of this," he assured her, and jogged to his car to get the spare from his trunk. He had to push aside boxes of papers, an easel with a few canvases, and a bag of canned goods he had forgotten about from the last trip he made to the grocery store.

"I had no idea you painted," Amanda said. Her voice was no longer filled with tears—now it was filled with delighted surprise. Jordan turned to see her standing behind him, looking as though she wanted to help but had no idea how.

"I paint from time to time," he told her. "I like having my own art on my walls at home. It makes me feel—"

Less lonely, he was going to say, but he stopped the words.

"It gives me a feeling of satisfaction," he said instead.

"Like baking a loaf of bread."

Jordan stopped with the tire halfway out of the trunk and looked at her. She shrugged. "I mean, that's what I would think it would feel like. Like baking a loaf of bread. I put so much work into it and then I smell it baking, and when I pull it out of the oven and it's perfect, it makes me think I can do almost anything. Is that weird?"

Jordan smiled. "No. It's just the way worthwhile things should be, I think."

Amanda caught the easel before it fell to the pavement. The wind had picked up, heralding the approaching coastal storm. Jordan hauled the tire to the ground. It bounced once before it rolled away from him in a perfectly straight line. He gave it a push toward Amanda's car. After searching under more papers, he pulled out the jack and the tools he would need to change the tire. Amanda watched him intently until closed the trunk.

"Thank you," she said abruptly. She was on the verge of tears again, but something in the set of her jaw said she would not let them fall. Jordan was touched by her fierce, young pride.

"You're welcome."

She nodded and together, they ambled toward her car. Jordan studied her out of the corner of his eye. Upon closer inspection, he wondered if she had been sleeping well. The dark circles under her eyes weren't quite hidden by her makeup, and her mouth looked tired. Many college students looked that way after a hard night of partying, but Jordan knew that wasn't the case with Amanda.

He wasn't sure how to broach the subject of her mother without upsetting her again, so he kept silent. Years of teaching had taught him patience. Amanda would talk, but it had to be in her own time.

Jordan dropped to his knees and placed the jack.

"Can I help?"

Jordan looked up at her. The sun was on its downward track across the sky, and shone from behind Amanda. In shadow, she looked even younger than she really was.

"You can sit there and talk to me," he invited.

Amanda sank to the ground beside the car. She crossed her legs and leaned back on her hands. Jordan started working the nuts on the tire, one at a time. It took some effort, and he was completely engrossed in the job when Amanda asked him, "Why did you decide to be a teacher?"

Jordan blinked at the tire while he thought about it. "Most students don't ask me that."

"School is over for the day," Amanda said. "So I'm not really a student."

Jordan looked at her sharply, but Amanda was looking at the tire. Her eyes were tired, and she didn't look manipulative. The innuendo he thought he heard in her tone must have been completely imagined.

This is what happens when you've been alone too long, Jordan thought. *You imagine the unimaginable in everything.*

"I guess it started in high school," he said. "I was the one nobody really knew what to do about. I was the one who never did his homework but got perfect scores on the tests. I was belligerent and headstrong. I was the one who stayed out all night and made my parents sick with worry, then came to school drunk and hit on the homeroom teacher."

Amanda chuckled, but the sound was filled with more sympathy than anything else.

"All the teachers gave up on me, and I guess I didn't blame them. But there was one who didn't. His name was Mr. Harrell."

Jordan popped the end of the wrench and the nut made a grinding sound before it broke free. He went on to the next one.

"Mr. Harrell pulled me aside one morning when I was still hung over from the night before. He didn't lecture me. He gave me two aspirin and led me to his office and gave me a pillow and told me to take a nap."

Jordan looked at Amanda. She was staring at him, intent on the story, her own problems forgotten.

"He told me he expected me to be ready for his class the next day. That he would cover for me this time. He said he wasn't sure what my problem was, but he expected me to be there after school to talk about it. If I wasn't too busy chasing women or booze, of course."

Jordan chuckled as he put his arms around the tire and pulled it free. "He was the only one brave enough to call me on the path I had chosen."

"What did you do?" she asked.

"I stayed after school."

"What did he say to you?"

"He listened to all my excuses. Then he told me I needed to listen to him for a while. And he told me what it was like to be a teacher."

Jordan rolled the spare into place. It was bigger than the other tire, but it was still good enough to get her to where she needed to be.

"He told me what it felt like to watch a kid bring in straight A's and then go on to an Ivy League school. He told me about the kids he still heard from years later, and showed me the pictures of their kids. He told me about seeing his old students in the grocery store, at the restaurants around town, everywhere, and how good it felt to be remembered."

Jordan rolled Amanda's old tire around so that he could look at it. He began going over every inch, looking for the trouble as he went on.

"Then he told me what it was like to bury a teenager who had just gotten his license and didn't have enough experience to keep it between the lines. He told me about watching some kids drown in their own low expectations. He had seen kids with bruises they lied about. He told me about students who had kids of their own while they were still children themselves. He told me about how often he stayed awake at night and worried about them, and how wondering about them long after they were gone from your classroom could drive you crazy if you let it happen."

Jordan found the nail in the flat tire. It had been there for a long time—it was worn smooth, curved by the road.

"He told me I was one of those kids. That he tossed and turned because of me."

Amanda was looking at the ground. Jordan studied her for a while—the long face, the long eyelashes, the steadiness of her breathing and the way she bit her lip, thinking hard.

"That was enough to light up my conscience. I was in class the next day. I didn't make it every day—change is hardly ever that complete and that sudden—but I made an effort. He never said another word about my drunken mornings or my wild ways. He just put his hand on my shoulder every time he passed my desk. Every single time."

He started to tighten down the new tire.

"I was on the fast track to hell. Funny how all it took was someone calling me on the carpet and telling me how my life was affecting them. I stopped being an arrogant jerk and started to think about someone other than myself. Every time Mr. Harrell dropped his hand to my shoulder, he reminded me."

"You do that," she said suddenly. "I've seen you. There's that guy—"

She abruptly stopped, and smiled in the sweet, knowing

way of someone who has a secret to protect.

"You're a good teacher," she said to him, and then it was Jordan who had to look down at the ground, away from the surprising tenderness in her voice.

"We've almost got this tire fixed," he said, and paid an enormous amount of attention to a job that didn't really need much attention at all. Amanda's eyes were on him the whole time. He wondered if he had said too much, but when he looked back at her to tell her the tire was ready to go, there was a look in her eyes that gave him pause.

"What?" he asked.

"You wanted to say something to me earlier. About my Mom and me. I wish you would go ahead and tell me now."

"You sure?"

"Yeah."

"I think you should pick up that cell phone and call her back and apologize before she has a chance to say anything."

Amanda raised an eyebrow. Jordan held up a hand.

"No, you haven't done anything wrong. But your mother is hurting so badly right now, she can't see the truth in that. You're still her baby, no matter if you're eleven or twenty-one or fifty. Right now all she sees is her baby leaving home, and in her mind, that means you're leaving her."

Amanda nodded.

"It isn't easy to put away the pride, especially during a tug-of-war when you're trying to make your own way and someone else isn't ready for it. But sometimes all it takes to mend a relationship is dropping your pride and saying the things that matter, which are not necessarily the things that make the most sense. Think with your heart, Amanda. Not with your mind."

Jordan released the jack and the car settled back to all four tires. He stood up and brushed off his khaki slacks. There was a spot of grease on the knee and even more grease on his hands. Why was changing a tire always so messy?

"You're all set," he said. "You can't ride on that tire for long, though. It's too big for your car."

"There's a used tire place on the way to my apartment," Amanda told him, eyeing the tire. "I can afford that. Is it alright if I wait until Monday to bring you back the tire?"

"Of course. Take all the time you need."

"I have another question," she said.

"Ask away."

"Why do you teach college instead of high school? From the story you just told me, it would make sense if you were in a high school."

Jordan shrugged and leaned against the car. "I did teach high school. For ten years."

"What happened?"

Jordan thought about how to answer that. He considered some trumped-up excuse, one of the feel-good answers that guidance counselors love to hand out to their students, but Jordan was a firm believer in the truth. Besides, he wasn't teaching high school anymore, and he didn't have to handle students with kid gloves. Amanda was an adult who was already in the adult world, so he gave it to her straight.

"Everything changes when you get divorced," he said.

They stood facing each other in the parking lot. Amanda had a way of looking straight at someone, her gaze steady as a rock. It felt as though she was assessing him from the inside out. Jordan hadn't noticed that about her before.

From anyone else there might have come platitudes, or a comment about how sorry they were to hear that he was divorced, or a commiseration about how rough it could be. Amanda simply asked, "Are you happy yet?"

It was a surprise question that made him pause. She didn't question whether he would be happy—she just asked if he was happy yet, and there was a world of difference in the two. Jordan could only answer with the same kind of honesty. "I'm learning to be."

Amanda nodded but said nothing. They both stood in comfortable silence until Jordan wiped his hands on his pants again and stood up to go.

"Well, I'll be going," Jordan said. "You might have a phone call to make."

Amanda smiled at him. "Thank you."

"See you Monday."

Jordan walked back to his car with the tools, watching his feet as they landed on the pavement, taking a breath with every other step. He could feel her watching him as he put the tools in the trunk. She was still watching him as he walked to the front of his car. He glanced back as he reached for the door handle. Amanda was sitting in the car, and the way the sun fell over the windshield, it was impossible to see inside.

Jordan started his engine and drove away, but her eyes seemed to linger even after he was far down the highway.

•

Jordan drove out of town, crossed the lake bridge and took the first paved two-lane on the other side. The two-lane turned to gravel about a mile out. A mile beyond that was a small one-lane road to the left, almost hidden by weeds. The gravel turned to hard, packed dirt. Jordan's house sat at the end of the lane.

He pulled up in front of the massive wood-frame house. This was his real project, the one that he didn't tell many people about, because they would have thought he was crazy to take it on—an old plantation house, without air-conditioning in the summertime and fireplaces for heat in the winter, plumbing that worked only half the time and electricity that was even more temperamental than that.

When he had purchased the twenty acres of land in the middle of nowhere, the house came along with it—and instead of tearing it down like he had originally planned to do, Jordan found himself falling in love with the grand architecture and the old-fashioned charm. He decided to move in and start renovating, a move that shocked even the real estate agent.

"You're going to live there?" she asked him once, about a month after he bought the house. He assured her that he was, and his statement was met with shocked silence.

"Well … good luck," she said dryly. He knew she thought he was crazy.

Jordan turned off the engine and the sounds of nature rushed in to fill the empty space. This was the moment he loved most about coming home. The birds trilled from the huge oak and maple trees that surrounded the place. Crickets called to each other from the fence rows. The breeze shuddered through the upper reaches of the leaves. From far away, a dog barked, the sound almost lost in the flowing of the long grasses that filled the surrounding fields.

Jordan looked up at the trees above his head, the wide maple leaves. "Heaven on earth," he said to them, and watched as they nodded in agreement.

Even the sound of his footsteps on the packed dirt driveway sounded comforting. He picked up the briefcase and made his way to the trunk to get the canned goods. He looked at the empty space where his spare tire used to be and wondered where Amanda was now—at her new apartment or making peace with her mother?

He swung the bag out of the car, picked up a sheaf of papers, and quickly realized he had gotten too adventurous. The bag ripped. Cans of peas and carrots rolled under the car. Jordan watched them go and once again swore that this time next year, he would have a garden of his own and wouldn't have to worry about canned goods in the pantry.

He got down on his knees. The smell of the grass was sweet and airy. He grabbed at the cans. One of them was close enough—the other was too far away. He cursed at it and decided to leave it there. By the time he got the briefcase, canned goods and other papers into the house, he was sweating and longing for air conditioning. Even the fans in the windows weren't enough to stifle the heat of early autumn.

He pulled out his cell phone and looked at the screen. No messages, no calls. He stared at it for a moment, as if a message might magically appear. Any minute now.

Outside the picture window, birds fought over something in the yard. The cat purred her way up to him and curled around his ankles, wanting to be fed. The grandfather clock in the wide foyer ticked. He stood in front of a fan and let the warm air move over him, which was only marginally better than standing outside in the hot sun. He looked down at the cat.

"Tell me I'm not crazy, Callie."

She blinked up at him.

"Tell me I'm not crazy for standing here in this big barn of a house and talking to a cat."

Callie yawned.

Jordan gently pushed her aside and went to the kitchen to open up a can of tuna. Callie started dancing around his feet, purring and meowing as hard as her little lungs would let her.

"Okay, okay. You're not starving yet."

He set the can down on the floor and Callie attacked it, growling and purring all at once. Jordan rubbed her back and watched her arch under his hand once before she was too interested in the food to bother with him any longer.

He put away the canned goods and went up the stairs. The air was even hotter up there, regardless of the efforts from the industrial-size fan going full-blast in the main hallway. The house would be a grand thing when it was done, but in the meantime, he was constantly reminded that he lived in a construction zone, and not a very hospitable one at that.

Forgoing the essays and the lecture notes and all the other things he should have been doing, Jordan stripped out of his school clothes in favor of old jeans and a T-shirt. He grabbed a bucket of paint and a brush. He carried it outside and once there, stripped the tarp away from a tall secretary desk.

He studied the nooks and crannies, and determined that painting the antique would take much more time than he had originally thought it might. He uncapped the bucket of paint with an old screwdriver and dipped in the brush. His hands were working, but his mind was a million miles away.

He thought about his parents, both dead ten years now, and the things he had put them through when he was a wild hellion back in his high school days. He wished sometimes he could take those things back, but then he always wondered if that would change the path he had chosen. Where would he be if things hadn't worked out the way they had, if the cards had been dealt in another way?

Jordan had minored in philosophy in college for one simple reason: He wondered why people wound up where they did, and if he had any choice in the matter, or if it was just destiny, with no wiggle-room for his own decisions.

He thought about his wife. No, *ex*-wife, as he had to keep reminding himself. Sometimes Jordan referred to her as his wife while in the company of friends and they all gave him sympathetic looks that spoke volumes. He supposed it was true that he was one of those ex-husbands who hadn't yet bought into the concept of divorce, who had been so deep in denial that the divorce papers coming in the mail were just another thing to be put away into a bottom drawer and left unopened until a later, more convenient date.

He had never opened those final papers. He already knew what they would say, had already seen it in his mind's eye and heard it in the judge's tired voice: This decree is hereby accepted, and the dissolution of your marriage is now final.

Jordan had seen the words like a neon sign in his head: Failure, failure, failure!

It was the only time in his life that he was grateful his parents couldn't see what had happened to him since they had been gone. It would have killed them to see what had become of him and Katie.

He watched the brush as the paint covered the side of the secretary. It was in a smooth line, just enough, done just right. He wiped his forehead with a sleeve and looked around at the trees. Callie had finished her food and was lying flat on her side on the ground, breathing steadily while she watched the leaves through lazy yellow eyes. Callie went with him when the divorce came. She was the only thing that Jordan insisted upon having. He was willing to give Katie anything else, but not that cat.

"She loves me even if you don't," he spat at her one night, and Katie had looked at him, her lips in a thin red line of dismay. But she hadn't said another word about the cat.

She hadn't corrected him about loving him, either.

Jordan shook his head to clear the memories. A drop of paint had splashed on his bare foot. Instead of wiping it away, he swirled it with one finger, making a small hurricane. The forecast had said Hurricane David was closer than ever, and might even turn this way. Though Jordan was a good thirty miles inland, he knew that wouldn't stop a hurricane from ripping through the marshland and wrecking havoc on an old plantation house in the middle of nowhere.

He looked up at the huge trees that surrounded the place. He would stay with his house if the hurricane did come, but where would he be safe inside the massive structure? The sudden vision of the whole top of the two-story house coming off with a ripping sound and flinging itself into the wind made him shudder.

"That won't happen," he said to Callie. She ignored him.

Jordan went back to painting and thought of Amanda. Where was she now? That was the only problem he had with being a teacher—he was the kind who needed to follow up on problems, needed to make sure things were set right, but sometimes that was impossible to do when you were dealing with other people who had their own lives. A teacher was a guiding hand, not a person who fixed problems. Jordan was a fixer.

Would he have reacted the same way Amanda's mother did, had he been the father of a young woman who chose to move out of the house and on her own? Jordan assumed Amanda's mother lived in town—why else would Amanda have called her for help with the tire? And he knew that most college students who had the option to stay at home throughout their school years did just that. Not only was it the comfort of the familiar, it was also the best option for saving money. It must have been a shock for Amanda's mother to see her little girl choose to fly the nest.

Jordan had never had kids. He paused and looked at the big secretary desk, imagined it covered with handprints and drawings, with little scrolls of crayon art stuck in a few of those nooks.

Are you happy yet?

He shook his head and went back to painting.

Callie looked lazily over at Jordan. She watched him, as she did almost every evening, as he lost himself in thought and found something to keep him occupied. She blinked at him before lying back down on the ground. She could feel the things that no human could, the way the ground was responding to the storm that was still too far away to be a bother, but soon wouldn't be. She shifted a few times to get a more comfortable position, but the ground just kept up that low murmuring, that promise of something monumental, whether they were ready for it or not.

A storm was coming.

Chapter Two

Amanda pulled into her driveway and cut the engine. The car rattled a few times before it gave up the ghost. Her apartment was a little walk-up behind an old lady's house, the kind of place where nobody would bother her because nobody knew it existed. That was just the way Amanda liked it.

She left her backpack in the car and walked up the steps. The third one always creaked, no matter where she placed her weight. The rest of the steps were worse. She carefully held the rail on her way up and once she got to the landing, she felt sturdy again. She unlocked the door and walked into her little apartment.

It was furnished with only the bare necessities. The furniture came with the rent, and that was a plus, because it allowed Amanda to buy the little things every tenant needs—a mop, a broom, trash can, dish detergent. The door opened to the kitchen and immediately to the left was the living room, with nothing redeeming about it save for the huge bay window in the corner, the one that Amanda sat in whenever she had a chance. The sunlight burst through that window like the sun itself was in the house, and was sometimes so bright that she had to pull the curtains in the middle of the day.

The third room in the apartment was the bedroom, and it was enormous. It could have easily been partitioned off into three separate spaces, and each would have had more than ample room. The corner held an armoire. Her bed sat right in the center of the massive space. An old chandelier hung from the ceiling. It didn't work, but sometimes the light came through the rear windows in just the right way and made the fake crystals look real, made prisms of light shoot through the room like rainbows of living color.

The bathroom was off the corner of the bedroom, a very small space that had little room for much more than the toilet and the bath. The bath was a luxury, though—a wide, deep claw-footed tub took up most of the space, but its old-fashioned charm seemed to make up for all the space it took away from the room. Amanda loved to sink beneath the bubbles and lie there for as long as she could, until her lungs began to fight for air, and then she would break the surface, panting. The water whistled through the pipes whenever she turned it on.

Amanda looked over the little space now and smiled. It wasn't much, but it was her own, and she loved being there. The first time she had opened the mailbox and saw her name on a piece of mail—junk mail, at that. She had laughed and danced all the way back to the apartment, not even caring that the wooden steps creaked ominously, not caring that the electricity was almost past due, not caring that there was a terrible draft around one of the windows. She noticed nothing but her name and her new address.

She found an old frame, one that she had left in a cardboard box during the unpacking, one that had set on her dresser at home, and framed the letter from the credit card company. It was a silly thing to do, a childish thing, but even weeks after the fairytale had started to wear thin and reality had crept in to take its place, Amanda couldn't take that picture frame down.

She stared at it now as she stripped off her clothes and listened to the water running, filling up that big bathtub. It was one of the small pleasures of having her own place—she could walk around naked if she so chose. The newness of the freedoms hadn't yet worn off.

She wished she had a few friends to celebrate with her, but the friends she had were few and far between. She never really fit in with the other kids during her years of high school, and she wasn't sure why. Perhaps it was her independent streak, or maybe it was the fact that she wasn't into the usual high school things. She didn't care a whit about makeup or fashion. She saw the prom as an excuse to spend way too much money, and she focused on her studies, not on dates or going out to the mall with the girls her age.

She didn't really fit in with the people she worked with, either. Her job at a major department store kept her busy, and she loved interacting with the customers who came through her check-out line, but never had anyone to really talk with during her lunch break. There were so many little cliques, and she was never quite a part of any of them. That was fine with her. She would rather sit with her lunch and a good book than talk about the latest gossip rags.

Things hadn't changed when she got to college. The other young women she was most comfortable with were those who studied hard and didn't have much time for anything else. As a result, she had only a handful of serious friends and no one she really called a best friend. She was a loner at heart, which probably had a lot to do with why she had moved out of her mother's house as soon as she was financially stable enough to do so. She needed her own space.

She wasn't just a loner. She was, as her father had once called her, an old soul.

She gazed out the window as she waited for the bubbles in the tub to rise. The leaves on the trees were moving with a constant wind. That wind seemed dangerous. She remembered growing up on the other side of town, playing in her grandmother's yard. Her grandmother would come outside in her faded housedress, always with a dishrag in hand, and look up at the sky. She could tell from the color of the sky what the day was going to be like. She taught Amanda how to look for the signs that even the most sophisticated radar systems could never quite pinpoint.

"You see that sky turn yellow, Amanda—that dull kind of yellow like the underside of a tulip about to lose its petals—and that's when it's a good idea to get a little scared."

She had been in love with the weather ever since. Now she wished she had a television set, so she could watch the swirls on The Weather Channel. Somehow it made her feel safe, to know that there were satellites up in the sky that would warn of the approaching storms, no matter how acute her own judgment might be. She would watch those swirls on the television as they moved inland and anticipate the first falling of the rain on the old slate roof.

She missed that sound. She missed television.

She missed her mother.

As soon as Dr. Eversole's car had disappeared out of the school parking lot, Amanda had taken his advice. She had made that phone call and as soon as her mother answered, Amanda had blurted out that she was sorry.

The reaction was just what Dr. Eversole had implied it would be—her mother had begun to cry, her anger melting away in the face of her daughter's contrite voice. The conversation was still strained, but it was filled with more understanding than they had had in the last several weeks, and for that Amanda was grateful.

Amanda walked away from the window and found her bubbles nice and ready, almost overflowing the tub. When she sank into the water they did overflow, and she threw a towel down to catch the moisture. Then she lay back in water almost too hot to stand and sighed.

She thought about Dr. Eversole.

He had been exceptionally kind to her this afternoon. She was sure that she would get some sort of lecture and have to bite her tongue to keep her defiance and independence at bay. It seemed professors either ignored you or paid way too much attention to you; never was there a healthy balance. Dr. Eversole had a way about him that made it clear he really cared about his students.

She was glad she had sought his advice, and he seemed to understand exactly what he was talking about. He didn't look down on her for her choices, or even try to change her mind, but he wasn't afraid to speak his own. She respected the fact that he hadn't talked to her like she was a child, as many of her teachers did, but like an equal.

He wasn't hard to look at, either.

He seemed strong. He was able to change the tire with hardly breaking a sweat. The muscles in his arms had worked firmly as he loosened the nuts on the tire. His hair was getting a little too long, barely touching his collar, a cacophony of dark curls tinted with a few strands of grey. His eyes were a pretty blue, the kind of blue you don't really notice from far back in a room, but once you see it up close you don't forget it. They were deep and intelligent and seemed to look right through you. They were the kind of eyes that gave you a moment of pause.

She had watched him and thought about how a person can look one way in a certain situation, and then look entirely different in another. As he changed the tire on her car, he didn't look like a teacher anymore. He looked more like ...

"Like a stud," she said aloud, and then chuckled to herself.

Her toes played with the stopper in the tub. The mirror was completely fogged over. Steam rose from the water. Bubbles floated up to her nose and made it itch. She thought about reaching for the washcloth but she was too comfortable. Her arms felt heavy under the hot water, and she curled up into it, almost like it was a cocoon and she was hiding from the world. Outside the wind picked up and a branch lashed against the window. She listened to it, to the whisper of the leaves and the crack of the wood, and then the sound retreated.

A bubble popped and tickled her nose. She listened to the wind and wondered about her elderly landlord, Miss Ellie, the one who lived downstairs and hardly ever made a sound, except on Sundays when she turned her gospel music up loud enough for Amanda to hear it through the floor. The old lady never went to church, but Amanda assumed she had her own kind of worship, right there with her record player and her gospel hymns, every Sunday morning.

Sometimes Amanda sang along, and a few times she could have sworn she heard the old lady laugh out loud at her sound of someone else's voice joining in with her own.

If that storm did turn to a hurricane, Amanda decided she would stay with Miss Ellie. It was the least she could do, and besides that, it would make her feel safer. Maybe she would invite her mother over, too. They could ride it out together.

She wondered again about Dr. Eversole as she played with the bubbles. She had heard that he lived in the middle of nowhere, in a big house that was practically falling down, and that he had gone a little crazy after his wife left him. Sometimes the more annoying students of the class made their snide comments about the professor rattling around in a house of ghosts, but even those comments were tinged with an air of sadness. Everyone liked Dr. Eversole.

What would happen to him during the storm? Would he stay in that big rambling house and ride it out? From what she had been able to gather from the gossip swirling about, he lived in an area that was virtually unprotected from storms or floods. It was one of the follies of the plantation houses in that area—they were built during a time when the owners thought they were invincible. Most of them had come down from the north for the promise of open land and good money, and hurricanes were something they had only read about in the newspapers out of New York and Chicago.

So they built their homes without a shred of sense as to location, and then paid dearly when the winds came and washed away the majority of what they had created. Amanda was surprised any plantation houses like that one existed anymore, but she was certain that if it was really as big as everyone claimed it was, the winds would have a field day with trying to rip it apart.

She finally reached out and grabbed the washcloth. The rough touch felt good against her overheated skin. She listened to the wind as she washed, humming a little melody. The faucet dripped every now and then, and she stuck her toe out of the water to catch the drops. They tickled as they ran down her toe and the underside of her foot. There was nothing she had to do this weekend. She was off work for a whole three days, glory be and miracles happen—and it felt good to sit in the bathtub and simply think.

Then she turned her head and saw the small boxes that lined the corner of the bedroom. Amanda sighed as she silently inventoried what might be in them. She did have some work to do after all. And once she was done unpacking those final boxes, she had to go over her finances and decide exactly what she could afford and what she could not. She knew the list of what she could not afford would be the longer one.

Amanda sank beneath the water. The bubbles popped lightly in her ears and then there was nothing but the silence pressing down on her, closing off all thought just as effectively as it closed off all sound. She stayed under there until her lungs ached, then she broke the surface in a flurry of bubbles. Water splashed over the edge of the tub. Amanda took deep breaths until her heart calmed down. She suddenly realized how dark the room had become, and how much time had slipped away since she had slipped under the bubbles.

Outside, a branch hit the window so hard it made her jump.

"It's going to storm," she said, and her voice echoed around her empty bathroom.

•

Jordan pulled another window closed on the east side of the house. Flakes of rust came off the latch and painted the old, worn windowsill with spots of auburn color. The latch was old, and Jordan had to work hard to get it into place. The glass was heavy—this window hadn't been changed since the house was built. The lead in the glass had migrated down, and as a result, the bottom of the glass was thicker than the top. It bulged slightly in the wooden frame.

He closed the one beside it and went through the same routine. Then he ran down the stairs to find cleaners and rags. He put these into an old bucket and carried them back up to the second floor, where he took his time in cleaning the windows. There wasn't much point in it—this part of the house was going to be remodeled next, and those windows would be dirtier than ever before he was through. But it gave him something to do, and made him feel less nervous about the ominous swirls in the Atlantic.

Callie was curling around his feet and meowing, even though he had just fed her a good breakfast. She ate half of his bacon and eggs, just like she seemed to do every morning. It was no wonder the cat was fat as a tick and lazier than that. Jordan rubbed back at her with his shoe and she purred loudly.

Callie had been acting strangely ever since Friday night. Jordan had finally fallen asleep around midnight, but Callie woke him up every hour with her intense yowling. Jordan had finally locked her out of the house, which made her yowl louder and had the added bonus of making him feel guilty. He gave up at five in the morning, when the sunlight greeted him with a strange, almost otherworldly hue of yellow.

Jordan found Callie sitting on the front steps of the house, looking at him with accusing eyes. He fed her and cuddled her during their breakfast, but there still seemed to be something amiss. The cat never quite relaxed, even when he rubbed her chin in that way that always made her go limp and purr with satisfaction.

He went over to the second set of windows. The wind was strong enough to blow his hair back from his forehead. A loud gust of it blew in a handful of leaves and set them skittering across the hardwood floor. Jordan pulled the window shut with an effort, set the latch and started to clean again. He was wiping off the windowsill when he heard someone knocking on the front door.

Jordan looked at Callie and she looked back with an expression of puzzlement that would have been amusing in any other circumstance. How had Jordan not heard the car? The surrounding land didn't muffle anything around the house—with those wide open fields, he could hear almost anything. Even dogs barking at the neighbor's house over a mile away were clear as a bell most days, as if they were right there in the back yard. Jordan could hear the cars passing on the main highway at night, if he really listened from the back porch. How had someone come up that long gravel drive without him hearing it?

He ran down the stairs with Callie at his heels. From the corner of his eye, Jordan caught a glimpse of green leaves blowing all over the yard. The wind had picked up even more since this morning, and he was surprised to think that it had been strong enough to block out the sound of a car in his driveway.

Jordan opened the door without bothering to look through the glass pane. The woman standing there brought such a shock, his smile faded and his welcome died in his throat.

"Good morning," Katie said.

For a long moment Jordan stared at her, uncertain of what to say. A part of him realized his manners were completely gone, but another, bigger part of him really didn't care. He had always thought he would be happy to see her if she showed up on his doorstep again one day, but now that she had, he realized he was not happy. Not at all.

"What are you doing here?" he asked.

Katie had her hair pulled back with one hand. She was looking slightly away from him, her face downcast to avoid the wind. She was dressed in a light sweater that was almost too warm for the day. The sunlight caught the golden strands in her brunette hair and turned it into an auburn fire.

"I came to check on you," she said. "Can I come in? This wind is horrible."

Jordan's first instinct was to close the door in her face. But then the manners with which he had been raised took over, and he opened the screen door. He had to hold it tightly to keep the wind from banging it against the house.

Katie stepped into the foyer and let out a long breath. She shook out her hair and looked around her, then back at Jordan. "Place looks good," she said.

"I haven't done anything in this section yet," he said, and she had the grace to blush.

"How have you been?" she asked, changing the subject already.

"Working. How have you been?"

Jordan knew he was being curt with her, but he didn't care. For the first time, the word *ex-wife* came to mind without any reminders necessary. He realized, as he stood there and watched her look over his house, that what he had mistaken for sadness was really a deep, simmering anger. He was angry in a quiet, furious way that would have stunned him, had he been given the time to think about it.

"I've been good," Katie said.

Jordan heard the grammar mistake and bit his lip hard to keep from correcting her. *I've been well,* he wanted to scream. *The word is well, not good, and why are you here, anyway?*

"Do you plan to stay out here during the hurricane?" she asked bluntly.

Jordan looked around the house and then back at her. "Where else would I go?"

"They canceled schools for the first part of the week," she said. "I thought you would realize how serious the situation is."

"They canceled school?" Jordan asked dumbly, then walked past her to the kitchen. There was his cell phone, plugged into the charger. There were a few missed calls, and one was from the English department. Certain no one would call him on a weekend, he hadn't bothered to turn the phone on when he got up that morning.

Katie stood looking at the new countertops. "Slate. Very nice."

"Why are you here?" he asked again, snapping the cell phone shut.

"You need to leave this house for the storm," she said. "That's why I'm here. I wanted to check on you and make sure you knew what was going on. I had no idea if you even had electricity in this monstrosity."

"In this what?"

Jordan stood in the doorway between the kitchen and the dining room. His hands were on his hips. Katie looked at his threatening stance and gave him that counselor's look of disdain. He knew it well. She had perfected it on him during their marriage.

"You know what I mean. This house is so old the slightest wind will blow it away. Once one part of it goes, so does the rest. Is there anywhere in town you can stay?"

Jordan stared at her, amazed at her audacity. Was she really trying to help? It seemed more like she was trying to dance on every exposed and raw nerve he had. Why would she come out to his house, after all this time? She had his cell phone number, didn't she?

"Why didn't you call instead?"

"What?" she said, and he immediately recognized the old trick. She had heard him loud and clear. She was asking him to repeat himself in order to buy time and think of a good answer, so he didn't say another word. He stared at her until she dropped her eyes and sighed.

"I wanted to check on you," she said.

"Liar."

The word made her wince, and Jordan thought that he had finally gotten through to her until she looked up at him with that haughty expression he had grown to hate.

"I wanted to tell you I'm getting married," she said evenly.

Jordan took a deep breath. The blow dealt by her words was sharp and deep, right in the center of his chest, and for a moment he felt dizzy. He leaned against the counter and looked out the window for a long moment, studying the way the leaves whipped in the wind. When he looked back at her she was studying him carefully, and he felt like a specimen under a microscope.

"Is this what you wanted?" he asked, his voice low and quiet. "You wanted to see the reaction?"

She started to shake her head, but Jordan saw the denial coming and cut her off with an upraised hand. She actually flinched back from him, as if he was the kind of man who would ever raise a hand in anger to a woman, as if he had ever given her reason to fear him. He fought the sudden, insane urge to laugh.

"You wanted to see tears?" he asked, the words bitter on his tongue. "Well, you won't get it. I've realized over the last few minutes that I really don't like you much at all, Katie. I especially don't like the way you manipulate people and then enjoy their reactions. You did that all through our marriage, but I was too dumb with love to see it. Are you happy with what you're getting this time?"

Katie was walking toward the door. Her heels clicked on the hardwood floors.

"You never change," she said.

"I don't have to change for anyone anymore," he said as he followed her. "I tried that once. I'm willing to bet the new hubby won't recognize himself in ten years."

Jordan was hollering by the time he got to the door. She was already halfway to her car, and there in the passenger seat was a man. The guy looked at Jordan with undisguised interest, and Jordan glared at him until he dropped his eyes. Katie slid into the driver's seat and said something to the guy beside her, shaking her head. Jordan could imagine her rolling her eyes.

"Whoever the unlucky guy is, he can have you," Jordan shouted at the car.

Katie glared and flipped him the bird. She backed out the driveway so fast she almost hit a tree on her way out. Jordan watched her navigate the full length of the driveway in reverse. She left a puff of dust in her wake, and it was quickly dispersed by the howling wind.

"Lovely," Jordan murmured.

Callie meowed from the ground beside his feet. She was hunkered down against the grass, looking up at him and then eying the sky with a worried expression that was almost human.

"You want to go into the house, don't you, girl?"

Before the words were out of his mouth, Callie had moved. She streaked up to the porch and scratched at the door. Jordan stood in the yard and looked up at the sky. The sun was shining and the sky looked clear, save for a few grey wisps of clouds that moved quickly across the blue canvas.

"We can handle this," he said, and he wasn't sure if he meant the approaching storm, or the news from the woman who was once his wife. He studied the sky for another few moments, then went inside to finish working on the windows.

Two hours later, Jordan climbed into his old truck. It was good for short trips around town but not much else. He bought it from an old man for a song because it needed work, but all Jordan needed the truck for was hauling the necessities for remodeling the house. The engine protested and whined all the way down the driveway, but by the time he reached the main road it was running smoothly.

The hardware store was out of almost everything he needed, but they directed him to the Lowe's just down the street. The manager there looked harried and tired, as though he hadn't slept in days. There was a long line of trucks waiting for plywood and lumber.

"It's really coming, isn't it?" Jordan said to the manager when it was his turn to load up.

"It's going to be a good one," the manager said, and Jordan knew he had said the same thing over and over that morning. The young man looked at a clipboard. The tag on his vest said his name was Mark.

"I haven't even turned on my radio," Jordan said. "The wind speaks loudly enough."

"They are saying Category Four," Mark said, and looked at Jordan with serious eyes. "I hope you got a sturdy house, man. Me, I'm stuck here in this building, but we'll be alright. I'm sending the wife and kids inland, though."

"Will it really be that bad?"

The young man looked closely at him. "You're not from around here?"

"I moved here ten years ago. I'm from Tennessee."

"We haven't had a good hurricane come through in the last fifteen," Mark said with a nod. "Even then, it was only a Category Two. I'm sure you've been through tornadoes, and you know how bad those are. This is almost the same, but the winds are constant and sustained. You might want to go inland, if you got a place to go."

Jordan watched as two burly workers loaded plywood into the back of his truck. For the first time, he was truly concerned about what could happen to his house—and more importantly, what could happen to him if he stayed in it and the storm was really as bad as the predictions said it would be.

"I might find a place," he said slowly.

"Would be a good idea, man." Mark was motioning to the next truck to move up in the line. "Hate to rush you, but—"

"No apologies! You've got a lot of work to do." Jordan jumped in his truck and gunned the engine. He waved out his open window at Mark, and the young man gave him a quick nod.

"Good luck to you, buddy."

Jordan turned onto the main highway and headed through town. He wondered about the house and whether it had been through one of the big storms in the past. He knew so little about the history of his land. He always meant to look into it, to put his research skills to work, but he had been too busy fixing it up to get around to looking into the history of it.

He turned onto a side street and looked at the houses on either side. Most of them were boarding up already. He watched a man on a ladder, nailing plywood over his second-story windows. A woman stood at the bottom of the ladder, ready to hand up the next sheet. Kids played on their bicycles, but the increasing wind made it hard to pedal. Another family was loading belongings into an old station wagon. A man was tying a tarp down over the top of the car.

"Getting out of dodge," Jordan said to himself, and wondered if he should do the same thing.

The wind was picking up even more as Jordan turned onto

his road. The water in the lake was whipping up into whitecaps, and the boats in the marina had been moved or were being tied down. The whole area was a bustle of activity.

The long drive to his house suddenly seemed very lonely and not all that safe. Halfway there, a tree leaned precariously over the road with every strong gust of wind. Jordan realized if he was going to leave, it would have to be very soon—the road would be covered with fallen trees if the wind got any stronger.

Jordan wondered about his students. How many of them would evacuate? Had evacuation orders been given yet? Where would they ride out the storms?

He suddenly thought of Amanda. She had moved out of her mother's house. Jordan remembered the look of defiance and pride in her eyes and thought that Amanda would be the kind to ride out the storm in her own place. He wondered where that was, and he wondered if her mother would be able to talk her into coming home. He wondered if she was safe.

He pulled over to the side of the road and stopped. He thought for a few minutes while the engine rumbled contentedly under the hood.

"That's pushing things a bit, isn't it?" he asked the windshield. "She's a student, not a friend. She's half your age. She's got a whole network of family and friends to take care of her."

But somehow, Jordan doubted what he had just said, even though he tried to logically convince himself. There was something about Amanda's attitude, something about her manner that made him wonder if she really had that network of friends after all. Why hadn't she called a friend about the flat tire instead of trying her mother first, knowing damn good and well her mother would be itching for a discussion on other things?

Jordan touched the keys in the ignition. He put both hands on the wheel and stared straight ahead, trying to talk himself out of a decision that had already been made. He looked at the clouds and then in the rearview mirror. The plywood seemed to look back at him from the bed of the old truck.

"Aw, the hell with it," he grumbled, and swung the truck

into a U-turn.

He headed back to town with the wind at his back. He turned down the side street that was the short-cut to the college campus, gave a token rolling stop at the sign, and pulled right onto the grass beside the Frost building. There was no one around to chastise him for it, and besides, he was in quite a hurry.

He jogged up to the doors as he found the key on his keyring. Within less than a minute he was in on the third floor, in his office, pulling out the top drawer of the big black filing cabinet. *Whitmore, Amanda Ellen.*

He snapped the folder open and scanned the front page. He flipped to the back. Outside, the wind slammed against the windows, rattling them in their old wooden frames.

"You hold your horses," he said to the storm, even as he found Amanda's change of address form. He had filed it away like so many other necessary but boring paperwork from the main office. He read over the address a few times to commit it to memory, then carefully put the folder back in the filing cabinet.

He started toward the door, then turned back to look at his office. He watched the trees outside the window as they swayed with the wind.

In sudden decision, he stepped forward and opened his desk drawer. In the little space in the back, there were shiny metal keys, rarely used. He pulled them out and locked up the filing cabinet. He hastily took all the papers from his desk and shoved them into an old box. He put the box underneath the desk. He snatched the picture of his parents from the top of it. Then he pulled the window shades, leaving the room in utter darkness. From behind them, the wind rattled the glass.

Carrying the picture under his arm and the address in his mind, Jordan left his office.

Chapter Three

Amanda stood at her window and looked at the tree. The branches that had been hitting the window had now snapped off, so the potential of broken glass was gone for the moment. But the storm was getting stronger, and soon the branches that appeared to be out of reach of that window just thirty minutes ago were now swinging dangerously close.

She clutched the keys in her hand. Her mother had gone to the inland and had begged Amanda to do the same, but she couldn't leave Miss Ellie. Amanda's mother had finally given up. She told Amanda that staying there was both a noble and a stupid thing to do, and she hoped once Amanda's new apartment was gone thanks to the storm, she would see the error of her ways and come home.

Amanda had hung up on her mother.

Now she stared out the window and wondered how long the storm would last. How long did hurricanes last around here? The last one they had was back when Amanda was too young to remember. She tried to remember what she had heard about it but all that came to mind were the stories of destruction. And that was only a Category Two. This one was a Category Four with the potential to become even worse than that, or so the forecasters claimed.

She had finally had enough of the view. Pulling her poncho tight around her and covering her head as best she could, Amanda ran down the stairs. Miss Ellie's front porch was covered with a wide roof and was blessedly warm. She stood underneath it and knocked on the door. There was no immediate answer, and Amanda assumed that the elderly woman was in bed or in the bathroom. She would come in a moment, surely. Amanda knocked on the door again, just to make sure she was heard, and looked out at the street while she waited.

The wind was blowing the rain in sheets. The gutters were already flowing with rainwater. The road looked slick. Cars were traveling back and forth, but not nearly as many as there were on any other day. Amanda figured most of the townspeople had taken the advice of the governor and had evacuated ahead of the storm. The college students who didn't have vehicles to get out of town had been taken away by the bus-load. She probably should have gone with them, but Miss Ellie had made it clear she needed someone with her, so Amanda had stayed. And just where was Miss Ellie?

As she raised her hand for another knock, Miss Ellie opened the door. "Oh, goodness, child," she said, all in a rush. "My brother Gerald just called and he's coming from downtown to pick me up and then we're going inland with the family. Do you want to come with us? It's going to get bad, they say, and I don't want you to be up in that apartment by yourself."

Amanda looked at her for a moment. Miss Ellie was leaving? Her mother was gone already, and that just left her and—who? The few friends she had were already gone. She looked at Miss Ellie in dismay. She didn't want to leave her apartment, but she didn't want to be alone, either.

"I don't know what to do," Amanda said. "I need to think about it."

Miss Ellie was taken aback. "Why, you're just a child! You can't stay here. You get your things ready and you come with us," she insisted, and turned toward the house, as if the conversation were over and done.

"I need to think about it," Amanda said evenly, not moving an inch.

The old lady turned to look at Amanda. She studied her for a long moment and chuckled at the fierce determination she saw in the young woman's face. "Come on in out of the rain while I finish packing my luggage," she said. "But don't think too long, dear. Hurricanes don't wait."

Amanda nodded and followed Miss Ellie into the house. She looked around the well-appointed dining room while Miss

Ellie went slowly up the stairs. The dining room table showed few signs of wear. The kitchen looked as though it had been well-loved, but it was perfectly clean. The living room was neat and the furniture was almost new. The house smelled heavenly, and Amanda attributed that to the pretty candles that adorned dozens of surfaces in the downstairs area. She made a mental note to get a candle for her apartment.

She wondered if Miss Ellie had anything to use to board up the windows. What had happened to this house after the last hurricane. Surely the damage hadn't been that bad, had it? After all, it was still standing, and had been for many years. She wondered if her mother had boarded up their house. Had she had anyone help her do it? If Amanda had been there, they would have done it together.

She could imagine her mom on top of the ladder, laughing and talking between strokes of the hammer. At the mental picture in her head, Amanda began to feel more than a little guilty, even though she was certain she had done nothing wrong.

Suddenly Amanda felt very alone in the face of the approaching storm. She looked at the clock in the foyer and calculated the time it would take to drive to her aunt's house. Her mother was probably there by now. She could pick up the phone and call her, just to make sure she was alright—

"So, have you decided, young lady?" Miss Ellie was coming down the stairs with a suitcase behind her. Amanda rushed to take it from her and make her descent easier.

"Such a good girl," Miss Ellie praised. "Are you going with us?"

"I think I'll stay right here, Miss Ellie."

The old woman sighed but didn't argue. "Fine, fine. But don't stay up in that apartment. Stay down here on the ground floor. You can sleep in my bedroom at the back of the house. That's the safest place in here."

Gratitude swamped Amanda. "Thank you, Miss Ellie."

Miss Ellie waved her hand dismissively. "Oh, bosh. Where's Gerald?" She was peering out the window at the road when the minivan pulled up. An elderly man got out and waved to them to hurry up.

"Get out here, Eleanor!" Miss Ellie's brother yelled, and

Amanda followed her through the rain to the van. The man took the suitcase and threw it in the back, and Amanda retreated to the porch.

"You stay safe, girl." Miss Ellie looked at her hard through the rain. "Stay in that house, you hear me?"

"Be careful," Amanda said, and gave a final wave. Within less than a minute they were gone and she was standing on the porch of the house, utterly alone. She watched as two cars passed, both of them filled to overflowing with what appeared to be all their worldly possessions. Their headlights beamed and their wipers were going full-tilt in the rain. Then a truck came down the road, slowed, and pulled to a stop right on the road in front of the house.

Amanda watched with curiosity. That curiosity turned to shock as Dr. Eversole stepped out of the truck and came running toward her across the rain-soaked front lawn.

She stepped out into the rain to meet him, and he immediately took her arm to pull her back under the protection of the porch. Both spoke at the same time.

"Amanda, you're not alone, are you?"

"What are you doing here?"

They looked at each other for a moment, each unsure of how to answer. Finally Amanda roused herself from her surprise and asked again, "Dr. Eversole, what are you doing here?"

He actually blushed. "Checking on you," he said.

"Why?"

Her voice was soft, yet the challenge in it was unmistakable. Jordan wiped the rainwater from his eyes. He considered his reasons why, then settled on the most obvious explanation, which also happened to be the truth. "I know you and your mother had a falling out, and I knew things might not be settled. I wanted to make sure you were alright."

Strangely, his concern didn't provoke her anger like her mother's had. The honesty of his words made Amanda smile, even though she was still scared to death and had no idea what to do. "I'm alright, Dr. Eversole."

"Please, let's not be formal right now. Call me Jordan."

His first name is Jordan, she thought. *Jordan Eversole*.

"Okay. Jordan. But I'm alright, really, I promise."

Jordan surprised her when he disagreed. "You're alone during this storm. That's not alright."

She thought for a moment. What did he want of her?

"I'm going over to the school," she said in a moment of inspiration. "They have shelters there."

He gave her a look that said he didn't believe a word of what she was saying. On the street, a car honked angrily as it made its way around Jordan's truck. For the first time Amanda noticed the plywood in the back of it.

"You are staying in that old plantation house, aren't you?" she asked.

Jordan's eyebrow raised in surprise. "How do you know about my house?"

Now it was Amanda's turn to blush. "People talk."

"They do, do they?"

They looked at each other and suddenly Jordan grinned.

"I'm thinking about staying in town myself, but I have to get back to the house and board up the windows. I also have to get Callie. You can go with me if you want. I could use the help, and I would rather not worry about you. Then I can get you back here to a shelter. How does that sound?"

Amanda nodded. "Who's Callie?"

"My cat."

The relief that flooded Amanda was definitely inappropriate, but she didn't let it show.

"Let me call my mother and tell her I'm alright. She's on her way to my aunt's house."

"Cell phones don't seem to work well right now, thanks to Big Bad David. Can you make that call from here before we go?"

She walked gratefully back into the house, and Dr. Eversole—Jordan—waited on the porch. Water dripped on the fine parquet floor in the entryway. Amanda wandered through the house until she found the phone, an old-fashioned rotary that sat near the stairs. She dialed the number from memory, and Aunt Marilyn answered on the first ring.

"Where are you, 'Manda?"

Amanda looked around the living room. Her eyes settled on the phonograph and the stack of records underneath it. That must be where the music came from every Sunday morning.

"I'm still in Sweetwater, Auntie."

"Sweetwater!" Her aunt's voice went from shocked to dismayed. "Amanda, this independent streak has gone a bit too far. You're staying there in a hurricane because you're stubborn, nothing more than that. You get in your car and get out of there right now!"

Amanda closed her eyes and took a deep breath. "I'm staying here. I'm helping a friend board up a house." It was true enough. She looked out the open front door, where Jordan was standing patiently and watching the rain.

Her aunt gave a loud puffing sound, which was followed by stony silence. Amanda let the silence build until she knew there would be no answer forthcoming, and she sighed. "Has Mom made it there yet?"

"No," her aunt said, with more than a little hauteur. "She called to let me know she's five miles out. The roads are jammed, you know. Five miles will take an hour, but she will get here and be perfectly safe."

"Good," Amanda said, then closed her mouth, despite the fact that she wanted to throw all sorts of words at her aunt. She knew her anger would do no one any good right now, and besides that, she was mature enough to know that most of her anger was borne of fear, anyway.

"Why do you insist on making your family worry?" Aunt Marilyn suddenly demanded. Amanda was so surprised by the question that she hesitated before answering.

"I don't intend to make anyone worry," she said. "Moving out on my own is not a capital crime, Auntie. I'm twenty-one years old."

Her aunt made that huffing sound again, then started in on Amanda with the full force of her tongue. "Twenty-one or not, you shouldn't have left your mother! It's just been you and her for years, and she depends on you much more than you think she does. She put everything she had into you after your father died, and this is how you repay her! You move into an apartment you can't afford, just to be on your own. You aren't even moving in with a man, which maybe would be more understandable. Your mother isn't hard to live with, but you've made her feel like she is. How could you make your mother feel so horrible?"

Amanda closed her eyes and tried desperately to keep some sense about her. Her hand clenched in her lap, and she pressed the phone to her ear so hard that it made her head ring. She took deep, even breaths. She wanted to yell at her aunt and tell her to shove it where the sun don't shine, but she knew that doing that would prove her to be the immature brat her aunt thought she was. Amanda knew she was more mature than that, and she wouldn't dream of giving her aunt any satisfaction of the haughty kind.

"I'm sorry you feel that way," she said simply. Her calm tone did what she feared it would—it sent her aunt into a rage of indignation. That a young woman like Amanda could hold her own in the face of the older woman and not argue with her was like setting a match to tinder. Her aunt's words went from harsh and clipped to loud.

Very loud.

Amanda pulled the phone away from her ear and looked at the receiver. She could still clearly hear her aunt as she yelled into her end of the phone. Amanda waited until she seemed to have quieted down, then put the phone back to her ear.

"I think it is best if I go now, Auntie. I hope you come through the storm alright. I love you."

Amanda hung up on the sound of her aunt's renewed tirade. She looked at the phone for a moment, then sighed heavily and laid her head in her hands. She fought for a moment to get the tears under control, unaware of the fact that Jordan was watching her through the glass.

When she stood up, he turned around as if he hadn't seen or heard a word. She locked up the house and met him there on the front porch.

"Ready?" was all he said.

Chapter Four

By the time they got back to the house, the rain had miraculously stopped. Jordan pulled the plywood out of the truck and stacked it beside the porch. He sent Amanda into the house, even though she protested.

"If you really want to help," he said, "Clean up in there a little bit. It's a mess."

"Woman, clean house," she intoned with a grin. "Man, hit nails."

Jordan laughed out loud as Amanda went into the house without another word of complaint.

Jordan focused on the east side of the house first, then worked his way around to the rest. He climbed up the ladder to the second story and was once again thankful that the house had a full balcony, so that balancing on a ladder in the high winds would not be required. He nailed up the plywood and Callie followed him from inside, darting from one window to another as she watched the work in progress. She meowed at him, and he blew her a kiss.

Leaves were blowing down from the highest trees by the time Jordan was finished. Despite the cooling wind, he had worked up a sweat. He was surprised by the darkness of the house when he walked into it after putting up the plywood. He was so accustomed to light and open space that the absence of it made him appreciate anew the architecture and careful attention to detail that the original builders had put into the house.

Callie stood at the bottom of the steps and gave a long, worried meow. Jordan scratched her ears.

"It's alright, baby. We're going to be just fine."

Amanda came around the corner then, a dust rag in one hand and cleaner in the other. "I've been thinking," she said. "This house is much sturdier than I expected. And it's been here a really long time, so surely it has withstood worse than this. Do you think it would be safe to stay here?"

Jordan breathed a sigh of relief. During the time it took to nail up the plywood, he had decided that he would rather stay in the house and ride out the storm. The building was sturdy enough to last through over a century of wind and rain—surely it would stand through this. And with him there, he could very quickly fix any problems, especially leaks in the roof, things that might cause serious problems if left unattended for too long.

Callie and Amanda both looked at him with wide, worried eyes.

"We're staying," he to the cat. "Get your catnip. Get comfy."

Callie looked nervously at the windows, somehow understanding they were to stay, clearly unhappy with the choice. Amanda went back to the kitchen, seemingly satisfied with the decision. Jordan went up the stairs, turning on the lights as he went. He wondered when the power would go out.

"I'm getting a quick shower," he hollered down the stairs. A strange feeling of unease came over him as his voice died away. He remembered yelling down to Katie to tell her what he was doing in another room of the house, one of those little traditions of married life. He hadn't had a woman around since then …

"Okay," Amanda hollered back, and then yelped when she knocked something over. Jordan grinned and the uneasy feeling was forgotten.

Even above the drone of the shower he could hear the howl of the wind as it fought its way around the eaves and battered against the plywood over the windows. His decision to stay was almost swayed by the sound, but by the time he got out of the shower he had convinced himself that staying was still the best idea.

Downstairs, he turned on the television. His satellite reception was spotty, but he saw enough of the Weather Channel to know there was major trouble ahead. They had correspondents out on the coast, video of dark, ominous clouds, and already the waves were washing over the beach and threatening the tourist traps.

"Anyone who volunteers for a duty like that has a serious need for an adrenaline rush." Jordan shook his head as he watched the storm knock the microphone from some poor reporter's hand. The guy chased after it, almost getting knocked down by Mother Nature in the process.

"It looks bad," Amanda said from behind him. She was sitting on the couch with Callie in her lap. The house smelled like lemon-scented cleaner and old wood—a comforting scent.

Jordan muted the television and turned on the radio. It was solar-powered with a backup battery, and he had a feeling that battery would get a lot of use over the next twenty-four hours.

"Time to get ready," he said to Amanda, who smiled at him nervously. "Sit tight."

He found flashlights in the hallway closet, and he also found an old oil lamp, one left over from his days with Katie. The wick was tall and the bowl was full of oil, so he knew he was good to go if the flashlights gave out. He found matches in the kitchen and put them carefully beside the lamp. The radio droned on and on about maritime warnings and flash flood watches and high-wind warnings. Jordan ignored it for the most part, until he heard something that worried him a great deal.

"Please be advised: A mandatory evacuation order for the coastal counties of Georgia is now in place. Counties affected include Brantley, Bryan, Camden ..."

Jordan had thought this might be coming, but he had no idea how hearing the actual words would make him feel. He stood up and paced the floor. Amanda sat on the couch and watched him as though she was waiting for a decision to be made. Callie appeared ready to bolt at any moment.

"Think we should go?" he asked Amanda, and she shrugged.

"It's a mandatory order. Doesn't that mean they can force us out?"

"I think it means we're required to leave."

"I've never been through this before. Have you?"

"No. We didn't get hurricanes in Tennessee."

"What say you?" Amanda asked the cat. Callie glared at her.

Jordan stood at one of the few windows he hadn't boarded

up and looked out at the front yard. The sunlight was rapidly fading, though it was only two in the afternoon. Even as Jordan watched, a large branch cracked away from the oak tree in the front yard and landed hard next to the rope swing. He watched the leaves shudder as the branch settled on the grass. A fine mist of rain had started, and the boards of the porch were slowly growing darker with the moisture.

He thought hard about leaving. What could he do for the house, really? If the roof began to leak or if a tree landed against a side of the house, he couldn't do anything until the storm was over. Any damage that would be done would just have to be done, whether he was inside the house or not. He was just one man, and what could one man do in the face of a hurricane? And besides that, he had a responsibility to someone other than himself. Why had he brought Amanda all the way out here?

He looked back at them. Amanda was stroking the cat, but it didn't do much good. Callie was still scared. She stared at him, unblinking. "You want to go, don't you?" he asked the cat.

Callie meowed, long and hard.

Jordan smiled and looked back out the window. "I don't know where we'll go, but we need to go somewhere, don't you think? I doubt we can get out on the highway with all the traffic. If the order is mandatory, they have to have shelters set up for people who can't get out. Maybe at the school. We'll be comfortable there, won't we?"

Amanda nodded solemnly. "I didn't expect to get so frightened when they called it a mandatory evacuation," she said.

"Neither did I," Jordan admitted.

Callie meowed again. Jordan went to the linen closet and started to gather up quilts and blankets. He found a change of clothes and threw them into a small overnight bag. When he came back downstairs, Amanda was tucking the flashlights and the radio into a backpack. He grabbed a few other things—his laptop, his school papers, the immunization records for Callie—and pushed them all into his briefcase. He grabbed snacks out of the pantry and cans of tuna for Callie.

Amanda found the cat's carrier. Callie climbed into it without hesitation, and Amanda chuckled at her eagerness. She didn't want to stay in the house a moment longer.

They loaded everything into the truck. The wind seemed to have died down a bit but now the rain was coming, and it was even worse. Every drop, propelled by the wind, stung where it hit bare skin. Jordan found a jacket and put it on, even though it was early autumn and shorts with flip-flops were the usual attire. Amanda was back in her raincoat. Callie growled at the storm as he carried her outside and put her in the car. She looked up at him through the metal grill of her carrier and meowed deep in her throat.

"We'll be alright. Let me get a few more things."

Jordan loaded up the middle of the bench seat with the blankets and necessities. Amanda climbed into the truck to soothe the cat. He pulled the convertible around to the far side of the house, where it would have protection from the brunt of the storm, and pulled the tarp over it.

He locked the back door and walked through the house, turning out lights and making certain everything looked as safe as it could be before he locked the front door. He hadn't locked the door in all the time he had lived out here and it felt odd to do it now, but it also felt necessary.

He looked back at the house, wondering if there was anything he had forgotten. His thoughts were cut short by a blast of lightning, the first one he had seen that day, and it was enough to make the hair on his neck stand on end. The sound of thunder followed a few seconds later, deafening in its intensity. When it was gone he slowly climbed down the steps. From the truck he could hear Callie and her constant meow. She was scared now, and to tell the truth, so was he.

The headlights cut through the driving rain. As he looked out the windshield, a piece of corrugated tin flew across the driveway. There were small bits of what looked like insulation hanging from the corners. Jordan quickly put the truck into reverse and turned it around, then headed down the driveway, all the while looking into the rearview mirror. He watched the house until it was out of sight.

Right before he hit the gravel part of the road, there was a cracking sound, almost like a gunshot. Jordan instinctively hit the brakes. The old truck skidded a little before coming to a stop. Then there was a roar, and a huge branch from the tree right in front of him fell to the side of the road. Though it didn't block his progress, Jordan sat there behind the wheel and stared at it. The branch was huge, bigger than he was, and if it had hit the truck, especially on the driver's side—

"If that had hit us ..." Amanda said, reading his mind.

"But it didn't," he said. "It didn't."

The cracking sound came again, and another branch came down. This one did block the road, but it was small enough that Jordan could easily move it. He put the truck into park and started to get out.

Callie yowled at him.

"I'll be right back, girl. We've got to get out of here."

Jordan stepped out and the rain hit him full in the face, making his eyes water and driving him back a step. The wind was blowing the rain and it was not yet a deluge, but soon it would be. He remembered the flash flood warnings and wondered how quickly the water could rise on this road.

"Stop it," he said out loud, trying to calm himself. "Stop it right now, man."

He walked toward the front of the truck and there was a moaning sound. Jordan looked up and there was that tree, the same one he had seen earlier as he drove the road in his truck, the same one that had just lost two branches. Something about it looked funny, almost as though it was at a ninety-degree angle instead of—

Jordan didn't bother looking anymore. He turned back just as the moan became a crack. It didn't sound like a gunshot. It sounded like a cannon. Amanda's scream of alarm came on the heels of it. The tree came down as Jordan hit the ground beside the truck. The force of the impact made the ground shake. The truck shuddered and rocked on its wheels. The sound rolled away like thunder.

Amanda was there, beside him, hauling him up to a sitting position. She held his shoulders and looked right into his face. "Jordan. Are you hurt?"

He shook his head. "I don't think so."

The truck had taken a glancing blow from the truck of the falling tree. The headlights still shone, but the engine had stalled when the tree came down. Callie meowed frantically from the front seat, but it was a cry of concern and fear, not of pain. The tree had fallen across the road at an angle, but there was no way to get the truck around it without going into the deep ditch, and Jordan knew the vehicle would never be able to climb out.

They would be staying with the house—assuming they could get back to it.

He looked again at Amanda. Her eyes were wide with concern. "I'm alright."

"Thank God. It was close."

"Too close. We have to go back, right now."

Jordan stood up and leaned in the driver's side door. Callie was looking at him with wild eyes. He pushed a finger through the mesh at the front of her carrier and she rubbed against it, but there was no purr forthcoming. She was too scared.

"We're going back home, baby. Just hang on."

Jordan climbed into the truck and tried to start it. The engine sputtered and the headlights flickered. For a moment he was afraid the engine had been damaged, but finally it caught with a roar and a billow of smoke from the tailpipe. Amanda echoed his sigh of relief. Jordan put it in reverse and went back toward the house. Callie stopped meowing when she felt the motion of the truck. Amanda chuckled at her.

"You know we're going home, huh?"

He backed through the wind and rain and pulled right up to the front steps. The first thing he did after he unlocked the door was take Callie inside. He opened the door of her carrier but she refused to get out, so he left her on the couch while he went outside for the rest of the necessities. Amanda came in with an armload of things and wordlessly put them on the kitchen table.

The power was still on. Jordan flicked on the television as he made his way out the door. When he came back, he realized the screen was black. The satellite was out for good, at least until the storm was over.

He placed all the bundles on the floor beside the couch and locked the door behind him. Callie looked at him in the gloomy darkness of the house. Jordan reached out to pet her and she allowed it, but she didn't arch against his hand.

"Maybe some food will work?" Amanda asked. She had an open can of tuna in her hand.

"Come on, sweet girl. Good food here."

No matter how nervous Callie was, she couldn't resist the smell. Jordan stroked her as she ate and looked out the kitchen window, one of the few he hadn't boarded up. The sky was dark now, and the leaves on the trees were blowing off as though it was the middle of autumn, not just the end of summer.

Amanda stood in the gloom and stared off into space, thinking things Jordan could only guess. She wrapped her arms around herself and took a deep breath. When Jordan caught her eye, she gave him a quick smile.

The lights flickered.

"This is going to get interesting," he said.

"It already is."

A few minutes later they were both sitting on the couch, Callie between them, listening to the radio and waiting for the storm. The wind howled. It sounded for all the world like a human sound, a ghost in the attic, a mournful woman missing her loved one. It meandered up and down the scale of pain until it settled on a long, hard wail that Amanda thought might drive her crazy if she had to listen to it all night long.

"How long do hurricanes last?" she asked. Jordan was fiddling with the radio. Many stations were clear enough, though the static under the voices made the wailing outside seem even worse.

"I have no idea. I know nothing about hurricanes, other than what I saw on CNN when Katrina came through New Orleans."

Amanda ran her fingers through Callie's fur. The cat had calmed down considerably, but every now and then she shuddered with worry.

"So you're from Tennessee," Amanda prompted.

"Yeah. Born and raised a few hours outside of Nashville. A little town called Paris."

"Like France," she said.

"Yeah. I think there are three towns in the U.S. named Paris. One in Texas, one in Kentucky, and one in Tennessee. There might be more, but I've been to all three of those."

Amanda nodded. "I haven't been outside of Georgia."

"Never? Not even on a spring break trip?"

"I'm not your typical spring break type."

Jordan looked at Amanda. She was studying the swirls of Callie's fur.

"I guess I know what that's like," he said. "I don't socialize much, either."

"Why not?"

He shrugged. "I've always been a bit of a loner. I don't really get close to anyone anymore. I played the social game when I was teaching high school, but since then I've gotten grouchy in my old age."

"How old are you?"

Jordan paused in turning the radio dial. He carefully turned it back just a hair, until the voice of the National Weather Service came in clearly. "I'm forty-three."

Amanda silently calculated the difference between forty-three and twenty-one.

"You don't act like you're forty-three," she said.

"How does forty-three act?"

Amanda shrugged. "I don't know. My mother is forty-five. She's very set in her ways."

"Maybe I am, too. I haven't had anyone around to tell me whether I am or not."

Jordan walked through the kitchen to the pantry. He emerged with a cooler, which he filled with ice from the freezer. He then loaded the refrigerated goods into it. Once it was full, he closed the lid and found another cooler, this one slightly smaller than the other. He packed the frozen foods into that one. He piled some food on the counter, mostly lunch meats and cheese.

"There's a loaf of bread," he said. "I think sandwiches are the cuisine for the duration of this vacation."

Amanda found plates and started to make each of them something to eat. She dropped bits of ham to the cat, who ate them with small, delicate bites. Amanda offered a sliver of chicken, but Callie sniffed at it and yawned.

Jordan was moving around in the pantry. He pulled out jugs of water and set them on the countertop. Amanda eyed them while she spread mayonnaise on pieces of bread.

The lights flickered again. They went out for a few seconds, then came back on.

"It won't be long before the lights are gone. How long do you think the power will stay out?" she asked.

"Who knows? Sometimes it goes out for a day or two for no reason at all. With all the lines down and the trees blocking the road, we could be here for a long while."

The power flickered a moment, then stayed, a steady glow.

Amanda looked at the one window that wasn't boarded up. The wind's howl had become so constant, it made for background music, something she hardly noticed anymore. She thought about roughing it without running water or electricity. She thought about making repairs to the house, about fixing whatever was broken. The idea appealed to her more than anything else had in a very long time.

"It sounds like an adventure," she said.

Jordan smiled at her. "You know," he said slowly, "I was thinking the exact same thing.

Chapter Five

By the time the afternoon rolled around, the adventure had taken on a slightly frantic edge.

The ceiling in the master bedroom was leaking. They realized this after a piece of gutter had come off the roof and sailed across the yard with a resounding twang. When Jordan went up to look out the window, he noticed the puddle forming in the corner.

"Amanda, can you help me?" he called down the stairs.

That's how she wound up in Jordan Eversole's bedroom, standing at the foot of the huge antique bed, thinking inappropriate thoughts about her teacher while she watched him on his hands and knees in the corner, spreading a towel over the hardwood floor.

"Can you get the paint bucket from the guest room? It's across the hall."

The first room Amanda went into was absolutely bare. The second one had paint supplies. A worn ladder rested against the wall. Lines of buckets stood at attention, all neatly placed with their labels facing out. She found the empty five-gallon bucket and brought it to Jordan. She enjoyed the way her footsteps sounded when she walked across the old wooden floors.

She moved forward and put it under the leak. The first plink of water in the bucket was almost lost in the roar of the storm outside.

"It tore off the gutter," Jordan said, confirming what they suspected.

"It's not like the gutters were doing any good in this," Amanda pointed out, and Jordan nodded as he looked out the corner of the upstairs window that wasn't boarded up. Even from across the room, Amanda could see how grey the sky was, how dark it was even though it shouldn't be nighttime yet. She turned to look at the rest of the room while Jordan contemplated the sky.

The bed was obviously an antique. The wood on the headboard was worn and scuffed. It was huge, bigger than most modern beds. The rails had holes in them. Amanda walked around the bed, studying the ropes that made loops through the wood. The posts were sturdy, solid wood, the kind of bed that would never be shipped out of a discount warehouse. She wondered idly how heavy it was.

The dresser matched the bed—simple, understated, obviously older than her and Jordan put together. The wood had been stripped down to its original darkness. The drawer pulls were mother of pearl and looked as though they might be the originals. The small night stand beside the bed was a mimic of the dresser, but it was obviously newer and handmade.

"Did you make this?" Amanda asked, pointing to the piece. When Jordan turned to look at it, his eyes lit up.

"Yeah. Want to see the rest?"

"Definitely."

With a willing and eager audience, Jordan forgot all about the hurricane raging outside the windows. He took Amanda out into the hallway and showed her one room after another. Amanda marveled at the original gaslights, the thick moldings, the fireplaces that fed into one another, so that a fire in one of them would heat the rooms above.

He showed her the breezeways, the wide windows that made the house so cool in the summertime. They looked at the hardwood floors while he explained what "tongue and groove" meant and why it was so desirable. She ran her hands along the hand-carved banister and gazed at the windows. On closer inspection, she realized the glass on the bottom was thicker than the glass on top.

She pointed it out to Jordan. "Why does it look like that?"

Jordan ran his fingertips down the window. Outside, the plywood shuddered as another gust of wind hit it. "The original windows were made with leaded glass. Over time, the lead migrates to the bottom of the glass. The more lead that collects at the bottom, the thicker the glass gets. Look how thin it is up here on the top," he said. Amanda's finger followed where Jordan's had gone.

"You can't replace this glass, can you?" she asked. She was understanding more and more about his desire to stay with the house and protect it as best he could.

"I could, but it would be extremely difficult. Obviously, no new glass would suffice, and I would have to find it from old estates. It would be costly."

They wandered into the bathroom, where a huge clawfoot tub sat sentry in the center. There was a modern sink built into a small closet, hidden behind a closed door. A modern toilet accompanied it, filling up the little space. The main part of the bathroom held the original sink—a bowl and pitcher on an antique base. A chamber pot sat behind a wooden screen.

"This is amazing," Amanda breathed. "You're restoring it and renovating it at the same time."

"Yeah. I know it's unusual, and that's why I love it so much. Most people would have turned all of this into a modern place, but I want to preserve the heritage as best I can."

"Do you use that tub? And that sink?"

"Yeah. Look how deep the tub is," he said.

She had to lean over the side of the tub in order to place her fingertips on the bottom. It was deeper than any bathtub she had seen, even deeper than most Jacuzzis.

"Wow."

"Yeah, wow. That's what I thought the first time I saw it. I had to keep it."

"This came with the house?"

"Most of the furniture came with the house. I bought some pieces up in Pennsylvania at antique shops. That rope bed came from there. It was really hard to haul up here. Every piece weighs almost as much as I do. The headboard weighs more."

Amanda stood up. She looked up at the chandelier and then over at the fireplace. The hearth was covered with a smoke-colored screen.

"Does Callie ever get into those hidden places and disappear?"

Jordan laughed. "Callie is too cosmopolitan to go anywhere that could get her fur messy."

As they walked down the staircase, Amanda glanced once more at the bedroom. She could see the corner of the rope bed from the vantage point at the top of the stairs. The bed was messed up, the covers thrown back, something she hadn't noticed before. Looking at it suddenly made her feel hot and flushed, as though she had been caught observing something intimate that was none of her business.

They came down to the bottom of the steps, where Amanda looked at the home with new eyes. She noticed how the modern couch had classic lines, how it fit in well with the antique table beside it. The rocking chair was old, but some rungs were new. The ceiling fan in the living room was obviously new, but the blades were of burnished copper, which gave the whole room an old-fashioned feel.

"You've done an incredible job," Amanda praised.

"You're one of the very few who think so," Jordan said. "Everyone else thinks I'm crazy."

"Crazy?" Amanda was surprised. "You're not crazy to preserve such a heritage. What does everyone else propose you do with it?"

Jordan chuckled. "Tear it down and build a nice ranch house with a big pool."

Amanda shook her head. "It would be a horrible waste of such a good thing."

Jordan watched her as she crossed the kitchen and paused to look at the dry sink. All this time, no one had really been on his side when it came to the house or what he wanted to do with it. No one else seemed to see the quirky nature of the place, the old-fashioned charm, the certain possibilities that were just a hammer and a nail away from becoming reality.

Amanda saw those possibilities, and she loved the house because of them. He could see the pleasure in her eyes, the way it made them softer than he had seen them before. She touched the antique pieces with a reverence that said she understood the age, and what a treasure it was to find something that had survived that long in such a fast-paced world.

She really liked the house. And the more he watched her, the more he liked her.

Jordan stopped dead in his tracks when that thought crossed his mind. It was time to straighten up and act like a teacher, not like a schoolboy who had a crush. She was his student, for God's sake. She might be of legal age and she might even be more mature than her years, but she was still his student—and she was young enough to be his daughter.

He watched her hair sway along her back as she turned to look out the back door. Her hand wrapped around the handle and she pulled it open carefully, keeping her weight against it so it wouldn't fly open without warning. Her body was slim. She wasn't very tall, but that seemed to fit her. She was small, compact, dwarfed by his larger size.

He turned toward the front door to get his mind back under control. What was he doing by admiring her form? Digging himself into a hole that was completely inadvisable to even contemplate? He had to be with her in this house for a while, probably for days on end, and he didn't need to be thinking thoughts that moved outside of the teacher-student relationship.

But when he looked back at her, he saw the hourglass shape of her body silhouetted against the storm, and thought that maybe he had already given things too much thought, after all.

"It's getting rough," she said, almost to herself.

"Close that door. You could get hurt."

The tone of his voice made Amanda turn around. He was looking anywhere but at her, and the words that had come out of his mouth were bona-fide professor. He looked as though he was contemplating lecture notes.

"Jordan?"

The use of his first name struck him, as though he was hearing it for the first time. He had told her to call him that, hadn't he? Why in the world had he done something like that?

Jordan sank down on the couch. He ran his hands through his hair. "I'm nervous," he admitted, and that much was the honest truth. "I don't like not being able to see what's going on."

"Like the Weather Channel, you mean?"

"Yeah. I went through a few tornadoes in Tennessee. One

of them was pretty big—wiped out the whole town of Jackson. There were storms everywhere that night. The power was out for a while. I hated that feeling of not being able to see what was happening. Have you ever noticed that tornadoes hit at night, when everyone is sleeping? They hardly ever hit during the day. I wonder why that is?"

Amanda locked the door. "It's something about the temperatures. They gain strength with solar power and feed on condensation. Most of them form in the afternoon and evening hours."

"Is that true?"

"I think so. At least, I think I remember it correctly. If we had an internet connection, I would look it up," she said.

Jordan leaned back on the couch and closed his eyes. He tried to listen to the wind and let it control all his thoughts. He knew Amanda was watching him, but he didn't move.

"Internet doesn't work out here," he said.

"I'm surprised the electricity does." As if on cue, the overhead light flickered, then went out. The house was plunged into darkness.

"Holy hell," Amanda said in surprise, and Jordan laughed out loud.

"It's your fault," he teased. "You should have kept your mouth shut."

They waited, but the power didn't come back on. The radio ran on batteries, and it continued to drone out one warning after another, naming the same list of cities and counties. The hurricane was definitely coming, and no matter where it made landfall, they both knew the house in the middle of nowhere was going to take a beating.

"Your mother," Jordan began, then paused.

"Yes?"

"She's going to be worried."

Amanda shrugged and wondered why in the world he would bring up her mother at a time like this. It was obvious she couldn't call to check on her, or go to her aunt's house through this storm. It would be days until she could let anyone know she was okay.

"She knows I can take care of myself," Amanda said.

Jordan said nothing.

"Jordan?"

"Yeah."

Amanda's eyes were adjusting to the dim light. She could see him on the couch, sitting where he had been when the power went out. She couldn't be sure, but she thought he might be looking right at her.

"What's with you?" she asked him, slightly annoyed and not bothering to hide it. She knew she couldn't stand the tension of hiding her emotions for days on end, so she wasn't going to start now. She had dealt with enough of that whenever she talked to her mother lately.

"It's just the storm."

They both knew he was lying. She considered pursuing the matter but decided it would be best to let it—whatever it was—blow over. She stood at the back door and listened to the wind howling outside, while Jordan sat on the couch and looked at her in the murky grey that was now the middle of the afternoon.

They were silent, listening to the dire warnings on the radio as the storm rolled toward them.

•

Two hours later, the storm had gotten worse. Amanda hadn't thought such a thing was possible. A tree in the front yard had snapped with a sound like a cannon shot, and Callie had dove underneath the couch, where she seemed determined to stay for the duration. They decided to leave her there, reasoning that she would be safer under there anyway, and from time to time they each cooed reassurances at her.

It was the only way they had of reassuring themselves.

The storm was blasting the house from all sides. Winds ripped at plywood. Shingles tore from the roof as their nails were wrenched from their moorings. Water dripped from a half dozen spots in the upstairs floor. Jordan and Amanda would no sooner get a bucket under one drip than another one would appear. Now it seemed the rain had subsided a bit but the wind was making up for the absence.

They huddled together on the staircase, side by side, both staring down at the foyer. Every now and then the wood underneath them trembled as with an earthquake. The constant hum had both of them on edge. Amanda was reminded of an old movie she had seen on late-night television, when continuous sound had driven a man insane. She mentioned it to Jordan, who gave her a quick look in response, but said nothing.

He hadn't said much of anything all afternoon. Amanda knew he was worried about his house. Hell, *she* was worried about his house. But she also knew it was something more than that, and wondered what it would take to bring him out of his shell. He seemed almost formal around her, holding back comments when he obviously wanted to talk, reminding her to check things she had already checked a dozen times, treating her like …

She looked at him in the thin beam of the flashlight. He rubbed his eyes.

Sunlight had completely disappeared hours ago, but if her watch was to be believed, it was just now time for the sunset. Without the flashlights in their hands and the oil lamp on the kitchen table, the darkness would have been absolute.

"Jordan?"

He looked at her, his face tired, his eyes guarded. "Yes."

She decided to be blunt. "Why are you treating me like a student?"

He blinked at her, surprised, then answered: "Because you are one."

The truth washed over her like the wind outside the house, and she looked away from him, unsure of how to respond. The blood pounded through her veins, so much harder than it had when it was just fear of the storm around them. This was different, a kind of heady anticipation that made her suddenly gasp for breath.

She stood up. Jordan reached for her wrist, pulling her back. They stood there like that for the longest time, as Jordan gave in to what Amanda was just now realizing.

"I'm trying …" He paused. "I'm trying to do the right thing."

"I shouldn't be here," she said.

Jordan took a while in answering.

"No. But you are and I …"

"You don't have to say it."

Amanda pulled her wrist out of his grasp and headed down the stairs, pausing to look out the back window at the nothingness beyond it. Jordan shifted on the steps behind her, and she saw his light flicker off out of the corner of her eye, but she didn't turn around.

On the heels of realization came the crashing reality—he might be interested right now, but look at the situation they were in. After the storm was over, the roles would continue, the same as they always had been. She was a student. He was a teacher. He had responsibilities and other things to consider, and he was going to keep her at arm's length until this storm was over, and then he would go back to treating her just like he treated anybody else.

"Amanda," he started, but she cut him off.

"I understand," she said softly. "It's the storm. The close proximity. The danger. It all makes things look different than they do in the light of day."

"No," he said, and this time, there was no formality in his voice, no distance at all. "Amanda, it's not the storm. It's you."

She leaned her forehead against the glass of the back door. It was cool against her forehead, thrumming with the force of the wind. She took in a deep breath and held it until her lungs threatened to burst, then let it out slowly, clearing her head as well as she could.

"I'm sorry," Jordan murmured, and she turned around to look at him in the narrow beam of light. He was looking at the floor, not venturing even a glance in her direction. "I'm totally in the wrong here. I know that. You have every right to drop out of my class, or to go to the Dean with this, or to feel uncomfortable from this point on, and I'm sorry I ever made you feel that way."

"How do you know how I feel?"

Jordan looked up, startled not only by the words, but by the emotion behind them. Amanda sounded like she was on the verge of tears. He watched her in the shadows as she walked toward him, her hand outstretched to catch herself before she ran into anything, her eyes focused on him. She came to within arm's length before she stopped.

"How do you know how I feel?" she asked again.

Jordan shook his head as he looked at her. "We don't have to talk about this …"

"How do you think I feel?"

Her voice was low, quiet, inviting him to answer.

"I'm your teacher. I'm too old for you. You're too young for me. I move in a different world, one that has nothing to do with college parties or frat houses or even most things people consider modern. I got you into a bad situation, and now you're trapped in this house and you can't leave, and hell, Amanda, you could die here, you know? It's a distinct possibility if this storm gets any worse."

"Who says I want to leave?" she asked.

"What?"

"You heard me."

"Amanda …"

"You forgot the most important part of that little speech, Jordan."

He swallowed hard. "What's that?"

"I'm trapped in this house with you."

Jordan stared at her as she reached out and brushed a lock of hair behind his ear. The gesture was so simple, so tender, that all of Jordan's defenses melted away.

She stepped into his arms.

The wind howled outside, but neither of them heard it. Amanda dropped her flashlight and it rolled across the old floor, making an arc of light under the counter. She wrapped her arms around his neck just as his hands came to settle on her waist, pulling her tight against him.

The first touch of their lips made the storm seem like a distant memory. She twined her fingers through his hair, keeping him close, letting him taste every corner of her mouth. Jordan's heart pounded as he angled his head, tasting her deeper, awed at the way she offered herself up, as though kissing him was the only thing in the world she wanted. He twined his fingers through her hair and she sighed against his jaw.

"We shouldn't be doing this," he murmured, trying to find one ounce of common sense.

"I know."

Her unexpected agreement brought him up short. "Then why are we?"

She smiled then, a glorious smile he could see even in the murky darkness. "Blame it on the hurricane," she whispered, the final word lost against his lips as he kissed her again.

Chapter Six

"Jordan, stop." She was laughing even as she pushed him away. They were on the couch. Pillows had slid to the floor and once they had knocked the radio from the end table, turning it to loud static, which they both ignored.

Amanda sat up and took deep breaths, trying to calm her racing heart. Jordan laid back behind her, his hands tracing her bare back while she tried to focus on something, anything, that would keep her from doing something they might both regret.

But God, she wanted to. How she wanted to!

Jordan leaned forward and kissed the small of her back. "Listen," he murmured.

Amanda listened, not sure what she was supposed to hear at first. She had almost forgotten there was a storm raging outside the windows. When she focused on it, she heard what Jordan had—the absence of wind.

"Is it over?"

"I think it is."

"It's not the eye of the storm? It's supposed to get worse after the eye goes over ..."

"The eye went over already," he assured her.

Amanda stood up and pulled her blouse around her. She could hardly see the dim glow from the oil lamp in the kitchen, but her eyes had adjusted well enough to the darkness. She walked carefully to the back door and opened it to find sheets of rain pouring down. She reached out to it, let the drops run over her palm.

"No wind," she said, just as Jordan snuck up behind her and wrapped his arms around her waist. "Hey ..."

He kissed her neck, rocking from side to side with her as they watched the rain.

"Amanda."

She smiled but didn't turn around, too content to feel his lips on her skin. She felt as though she could stand there forever, between him and the rain.

"Amanda."

"Hmm?"

"Are you sleepy?"

She wasn't sleepy until he said the words, but as soon as the thought of rest entered her mind, her body wanted to give out. How long had they been trapped in the house? Time seemed to bend around itself, so that she didn't know if it had been hours or days.

"I'm exhausted," she admitted.

"Then come to bed."

The idea of going up those stairs, of crawling under the covers of that big bed with him, made her anything but sleepy.

"Is that a good idea?"

He laughed, his voice kind as he nibbled on her earlobe. "I won't take advantage of you. I swear."

"You're not a good liar, professor."

He smiled against her shoulder.

"Come to bed."

Real doubts began to assail her, and she fought for what to say. "Jordan ..."

He turned her around to face him. In the dim light of the oil lamp, he looked just as tired as she felt, but his eyes were bright, alive with passion.

"I'm serious. There's nothing we can do for the house while it's dark, so there's no point in staying up. If we keep making out on my couch, we're both going to fall asleep in the middle of it anyway, and that does nothing at all for my confidence, you know?"

Amanda laughed and wrapped her arms around him.

"You won't try to seduce me?" she purred.

"I've been seducing you all night."

"You've been doing a fine job."

"But I won't push you."

Amanda laid her head on his shoulder. "Going to bed sounds good."

They made their way up the stairs. Amanda loved the way the steps creaked under their weight, and the way the wide staircase could allow both of them to go up side by side, holding hands.

In the bedroom, rain plunked down into a bucket in the corner. The sound of it on the roof was a quiet roar. Jordan kicked off his jeans and climbed into bed, then reached for Amanda's hand.

"Sleep beside me, Amanda."

She slipped under the sheets. He pulled her up close to him, pressed his bare chest against her back, and pressed his hand against the gentle curve of her belly. Lying together on the same pillow in that antique bed, neither of them had time to give another thought to the pleasures of the flesh. Within seconds, both of them were sound asleep.

•

When Jordan pulled the first piece of plywood from the windows, sunlight poured in. It almost blinded Amanda as she came out of the bathroom, her hair still wet from her bath, wrapped in one of Jordan's shirts. The cotton smelled like him, came down past her knees and made her feel undeniably sexy.

Jordan looked in the window and smiled at the sight. "You're beautiful," he called through the glass.

"You're a mess," she answered, laughing. His hair was flattened on one side and spiked on the other. He sorely needed a shave.

"I was too tired of living in that darkness," he said. "Light! I must have light."

With that he went to the next window. Amanda listened as the nails squealed against his hammer, as the sliver of light began at the top and the plywood came loose. She found her jeans in the corner, thrown there sometime during the morning, and she smiled as she picked them up. She slowly put them on, then grabbed a pillow from the floor and lay down on the bed to watch Jordan work.

The second piece of plywood hit the ground below with a hollow thud. Callie raced into the bedroom and stuck her tiny nose against the window, happy to be able to see the outside again. Jordan teased her through the glass, then moved to the final piece of plywood outside the bedroom. Amanda looked at the wide windows, amazed they made it through the winds intact.

Surprisingly, every window on the upper stories had survived admirably through the storm. The east side of the house had a few small panes that would have to be replaced, but that was better than the alternative. When Jordan was finished with the windows, he climbed back into the house through the master bedroom and found Amanda sound asleep on the bed, her arms wrapped around his pillow, her body covered with one of his old shirts.

The sight of her there took his breath away. He moved quietly so as not to disturb her, and sat down in the high-backed chair in the corner. He watched her breathe, watched the sun play with her hair, enjoyed the way her lips looked in the light of day, swollen from his kisses. She shifted once and began to snore lightly, a sound that made Jordan smile.

He knew how much work there was to do. From outside the house, the world looked ominous. Trees were down everywhere. Shingles had ripped from all sides of the roof, and in some places the protective covering underneath had been ripped away, exposing the wood.

The power lines that usually ran from the pole in the far corner of the property were nowhere to be seen. His truck had somehow come through the storm with little more than cracked windows, but he was afraid to go around the side of the house to look at his car. Small measures of reality would be better than one big slam of it, Jordan thought.

But all those thoughts seemed to vanish as he watched Amanda sleep.

He knew what had happened last night wasn't the smartest thing, but it had seemed the most natural thing. He wasn't sure when he had stopped caring about what other people might think, or about the problems an affair with a student would cause, but it was true—he didn't care anymore.

The more he learned about her, the more delighted he became. The more they talked, the more they found in common, and the years between them began to melt away until they didn't matter. There was much more between him and Amanda than what the harpies would whisper about, and that was something that even the most ardent speculation couldn't crack.

But he was still her teacher, wasn't he?

That gave him a moment of pause. If word of last night ever got out, his job could be in jeopardy. It was a very clear rule, both unwritten and set in stone: Teachers do not date students. No matter how much they have in common.

Jordan looked out the window. He stared at the brightness until the sun made his eyes hurt. What would Amanda's friends think? Would she care? What if she thought of this as a fling, a passionate few days brought on by a passionate storm? What if all his worries were for nothing?

Jordan pushed that thought aside. If he knew Amanda the way he thought he did, he knew she was not the kind of woman to take such things lightly.

Amanda stretched and rolled onto her back. She slowly opened her eyes, rubbed her nose with the back of one hand, and sat up. She blinked a few times and when she turned and saw him, she smiled.

"Good morning again," he teased, and she blushed.

"How long did I sleep?"

"I was too busy looking at you to look at a watch."

She snorted with laughter. "That is such a line."

"Did it work?"

They smiled at each other over the space of the bedroom.

"Come here," she said.

Jordan wrapped his arms around her as he dropped to the bed. They lay together and looked out the window at the clear blue sky, unmarred by a single cloud.

"It's hard to believe," she said. "Looking out there, it's like the hurricane never happened at all."

"You haven't seen the ground yet."

She looked at him with wide eyes. "It's bad?"

"Not as bad as it could have been, but we still have a lot of work to do. You game?"

She gave him a crooked grin. "I'm in this for the long haul."

Jordan stared at her, unmoving. She realized what she had

said, and a scarlet blush stole over her cheeks as she tried to find a way to take back what she had just said. She wasn't sure Jordan wanted the same things she did, and she didn't want to push—

"Good," he said.

"What?"

"Good. I'm glad you're in for the long haul, and I hope you weren't just talking about the house."

Happiness broke through Amanda's whole being, as bright as the sunlight outside. "Really?"

"Really."

"You know…"

"It's going to mean a lot of issues to deal with?"

"Yes."

"I'm not going to tell you it's going to be easy, for either of us. But I want to see where this goes, Amanda. And to be honest, I haven't wanted to say that to any woman for a long, long time."

She smiled up at him. "Are you happy yet?"

The words took him back to the first time she had said them, in the college parking lot. Had it only been a few days since then? It felt like both yesterday and a lifetime ago.

"Right now, Amanda, I'm the happiest man on earth."

She pulled him down for a kiss. "Then the house can wait."

•

By the time they got down the stairs, made something to eat for lunch, and surveyed the damage, it was mid-afternoon. They started by backing his truck into the center of the yard and throwing in branches, one after another, until the bed was piled high. Smaller branches were bundled up into kindling for winter use. Then they drove the truck down the lane and into an open field, where they unloaded everything.

"It will make for a good bonfire later," he said. "Once all that wood dries out, we'll roast marshmallows over the flames."

She wiped her forehead and climbed back into the bed, yanking another branch from under the tool box near the cab. "I wonder how bad things are in town?"

"I'm almost afraid to find out."

"Makes you glad the power is still out, doesn't it?"

"I guess we could turn on the radio, but I like this right now. Don't you?"

She shielded her eyes with one hand and smiled down at him. "It's perfect."

Back at the house, Amanda was the first one brave enough to look at his convertible. She came back with a frown and shook her head when he asked how bad it looked. "You have insurance?"

"Yeah."

"Good."

They found things among the puddles. A child's rattle floated in the water. A shirt, once white, had ripped off someone's clothesline and taken a clothespin with it. Envelopes, what appeared to be a block's worth of mail, was scattered all over the yard, each with a different name and address. They stacked them in neat piles on the porch, though most of them were too wet to be of any use to anyone.

Amanda picked up a notebook and watched as the water drained from the tattered corner. "It must have been horrible," she said, looking at the stream of muddy water. "It must have ripped houses apart."

Jordan nodded and looked up at his own house. Afraid to think of what his beloved college might look like, he forced himself to think of anything else. "We've got time to do some shingles before the sun goes down."

Amanda dropped the notebook on the porch. "Lead the way."

By the time they were done with the roof, the first of the stars were winking on in the sky. They laid back on the steep slope and watched as the sky turned dark, then turned light again with the rising of the almost-full moon. They held hands and said very little, simply content to be together as the world turned without them.

"Tomorrow, I'll saw that old tree and clear the road," he said.

"Do you have to?"

Jordan smiled as he looked up at the moon. "Maybe it could wait one more day."

Chapter Seven

The second day was spent cleaning up the last of the debris and hauling out Jordan's car. The sight of the fine leather top ripped away, as well as the windshield shattered by a flying piece of God-knows-what, almost made him weepy. Amanda teased him about being a typical man in love with his toys, and by the time they had cleaned out the interior as best they could, she had cajoled a small smile from him.

That night they fired up the grill and cooked the food that was threatening to spoil in the absence of electricity to keep it cold. They feasted on steaks and burgers and drank tall glasses of lukewarm lemonade. By the time they were done, neither wanted to move. Their bodies were sore from all the work, their bellies were full, and their hearts were content.

The next morning, Jordan awoke with the sunlight, and Amanda woke to the touch of his hand.

"Do we really have to clear that road today?" she asked.

"No."

They didn't leave the house.

•

On the fourth day, Amanda watched from the hood of the truck as Jordan fired up the chainsaw and went to work on the tree that had promised them refuge for three days. Sawdust flew all around him, turning his dark hair almost blonde.

She watched the muscles in his arms as he wielded the roaring machine against the unforgiving wood, making it whine and crack as it gave way under the chain.

Finally the pieces were small enough to push to the side. Jordan would leave them there to dry and in the autumn, they would become firewood. When they climbed into the truck and looked at each other, it was with a sense of longing. No matter how necessary it was, neither of them wanted to enter the outside world.

"I wonder how my apartment looks," Amanda mused. "Miss Ellie's house might be gone."

Then you could stay with me, Jordan thought, but bit back the words before he let them go. Saying that might push her, and that was the last thing he wanted to do.

"Maybe it wasn't that bad," he said, but they both knew better, especially when they turned the first corner into town and saw the National Guard troops in their camouflage gear, their Humvees and trucks blocking the road. Jordan reached over and squeezed Amanda's hand as they came to a stop and one of the officers approached the driver's side window.

"Hey, buddy—rough few days, huh?"

"How bad did it get?" Jordan asked, and the Guardsman shook his head in answer.

"You from in town?"

"I'm from out of town, but her apartment is here," he said, gesturing to Amanda. "I'm a teacher at the college."

"Got any ID to prove it? Can't be too careful, you know. Looting got bad before we got here."

Jordan pulled out his wallet and showed the Guardsman his faculty card. Amanda leaned over and said, "We haven't had electricity for days. No television. How bad did it get?"

The man handed Jordan his ID and smiled sadly at Amanda. "As bad as it could."

Jordan and Amanda looked at each other in shocked silence. As the reality began to sink in, Jordan eased the truck into drive and moved past the checkpoint. Jordan carefully navigated the roads, dodging fallen trees and debris, sometimes moving at a crawl. Neither of them said a word as they headed toward Miss Ellie's house, but when they turned the corner and saw the devastation, Amanda couldn't hold back a strangled cry of despair.

The house was still standing, but that wasn't saying much. Part of the roof had been torn away, exposing Amanda's apartment to the storm. Even from the road, it was obvious everything had been saturated by the rain or scattered by the winds. Amanda sat still as a stone, tears in her eyes, as she looked at the place she had just started to call home.

Jordan touched her shoulder. She looked at the ruined building for a minute more, then turned to him. She went into his arms without a word. Jordan ran his hand over her hair as he held her, saying soothing things, but the whole time he was staring at the house, trying not to think of what would have happened if Amanda had chosen to stay there.

"Do you want to go up there?" he asked her.

She nodded, still unable to speak. They got out of the truck and moved carefully toward the house, aware of the lumber and insulation and shingles all over the yard. The refrigerator from Amanda's apartment was lying on the ground, door open, almost all the contents gone. The fridge was filled with almost a foot of water.

"Where's my car?" she asked, looking around at the mess.

"Under the tree over there."

She turned to see a huge maple tree lying on top of what was once her vehicle. The only wheel visible was the one Jordan had replaced for her. Was that really less than a week ago? She moved on to the house and looked up at the forlorn space that was her apartment.

"The steps are gone," Amanda said as they stood beside the house. "It is too dangerous to go up there anyway, Jordan."

He nodded. As much as he wanted to take control and take care of Amanda, he knew how determined she was to make it on her own, and he was trying to find a balance between offering help and pushing it on her. "What do you want to do?"

She sighed and kicked at a dresser drawer. It wasn't hers—it had to have come from someone else's house, though she had no idea whether that was next door or a mile away. "I want to tell my mother that I'm alright."

Jordan smiled in spite of the horrible scene in front of them. "Good idea."

"Let's go check on your office."

Amanda walked in front of him to the truck. She stumbled once, and Jordan reached out to catch her, but before he could she had righted herself and was too far ahead. In the truck she sat quietly, looking straight ahead, as he started the engine.

"Amanda."

She blinked at him. Her eyes filled with tears. "It isn't a good idea for me to hold your hand, is it?"

He immediately reached over and did one better—he pulled her into his arms. She came across the bench seat without an ounce of protest, clinging to his shoulders as she buried her face against his chest and let the tears go. When the sobs slowed down, he gently pushed her away enough to look at her face.

"Why?" he asked. "Why would you think I wouldn't want to hold your hand?"

She shook her head and smiled. "You're wrong, Jordan. I didn't say you didn't want to. I said it probably wasn't a good idea. People talk."

Jordan sighed and looked out the windshield. Dozens of people were combing through the rubble, picking up debris, salvaging what they could. "I don't care."

"You have to care. You have a job to protect."

He stared at her. "You have got to be kidding me."

"No."

"Amanda, for God's sake! You've just lost a great deal, and now you want to pick a fight? Do you really want to argue right now?"

"I'm not trying to argue," she said, knowing that was a lie.

"We'll figure everything out soon enough, but not today."

She started to argue but before the words were out of her mouth, the tears started again. "You're right. I've lost a lot. Suddenly I'm afraid I'm going to lose you, too."

Jordan pulled her harder against him. "I'm not going anywhere."

Amanda laid her head on his shoulder and cried until her whole body hurt. She watched the sunlight bounce from the hood of the truck and thought about how everything could change so quickly, how the whole world could plunge into chaos and then the sun would shine brightly afterward, as though nothing had happened at all. How could anything be the same?

"It's not fair," she murmured against his neck, not sure whether she meant the storm, or the obstacles she and Jordan would face if they decided to nurture what they had started.

"It never is," he answered.

•

The college had seen better days. Most of the buildings had sustained damage of some kind. The maintenance crews had boarded up many windows on campus, but ran out of supplies before they could get to all the areas. As a result, half of the windows were pristine, and the other half were shattered. Branches littered the quad and one of the old, majestic trees had been split in half, but the rest of them were surprisingly intact. Jordan pointed that out to Amanda, who shrugged and said she wasn't surprised.

"Imagine those roots," she said. "Those trees have been here for well over a hundred years. This whole quad is filled with root systems. In order to take out one of those trees, the storm would have to take a huge chunk of land out with it."

Jordan was not one of the luckier teachers. His window had shattered, and his entire office was soaked with water. The desk had been destroyed by a falling branch. The file cabinet had moved across the floor, but when Jordan pulled out the keys and unlocked it, he was surprised to see the papers inside

Amanda picked up some papers and put them on what was left of the desk. Jordan glanced at them. They belonged to the teacher whose office was two doors down from his. The wind must have been fierce enough to pull things from one room and throw them into another.

"I don't know where to start," he told Amanda. She knelt down and picked up a few more papers, then stacked them as well as she could on the desk. Even though it had been days since the hurricane swept through, everything was still waterlogged. Drops slid down the side of the desk to puddle on the only part of the floor that seemed dry.

"I guess we just start," she said, picking up a third handful and putting them on top of the rest.

"Hey."

Amanda looked up. Jordan was going through a file, a small smile on his face. "Whitmore, Amanda Ellen. Birthdate: April 21. Hometown: Chicago." He paused. "You don't sound like you're from Chicago."

She took the file from him with a smile, the first she had

given him since she had seen the devastation that was once her apartment. "Mom and I moved here when I was twelve. I guess I lost the accent over time. Mom still has it, though. She's got that northern twang."

"Is that when your father died? When you were twelve?"

"Yeah."

"What happened?"

Amanda was quiet for a moment before she closed the file. "Plane crash," she said. "Dad was a pilot. He flew commercial jets, but even on his off-time, he loved the air more than the ground. He crashed his little Cessna in a rainstorm."

"I'm sorry," Jordan said, and Amanda shrugged.

"I have good memories of him. He wasn't home much, but when he was, he was entirely present with us, you know? We had his full attention from the moment he walked in the door. Sometimes I see parents who don't spend any time with their kids at all, and it reminds me to be grateful I had so much time with my dad."

"I'm sure that was hard on both you and your mother."

"Mom fell apart. Understandably," Amanda said, shaking her head. "Can you imagine?"

"No," Jordan said softly. "I don't think anyone ever can imagine that, until it happens."

"You never talk about your parents," she said.

Jordan looked out the shattered window. He watched a student picking up debris, filling a huge black trash bag with it, bobbing his head to whatever music was piped through his headphones. "It was a car accident," he said. "Both of them at once."

"Losing Dad was hard. I don't know that I could have survived losing both Mom and Dad."

Jordan nodded. "My consolation was that they had each other. They didn't have to suffer through the loss of the one person they have loved for decades. They went together."

Amanda smiled at him. "Why, Jordan. You're a romantic."

He gave her a grin and turned away before she could see him blushing.

•

By the time the sun went down that night, Jordan and

Amanda were both exhausted. They had cleaned up his office as best they could, then gone down to the athletic complex, where a shelter had been set up. There, they helped as much as they could.

Jordan was given a toolbox and set to work on the school grounds, where he fixed everything he could with the materials he had. Amanda helped families fill out paperwork for assistance, then joined the line to serve dinner to those who had nowhere else to go.

Somewhere in between the piles of assistance forms and the meatloaf plates, Amanda called her aunt's house. The phone was answered on the first ring. "Hello?"

"It's me, Auntie."

The woman on the other end of the phone let out a huge sigh of relief, and then burst into sobs. She spoke to someone in the background, and within seconds Amanda's mother came on the line, her voice filled with happiness.

"Amanda, honey! Are you okay? You're not hurt?"

"No, I'm not hurt. I'm alright." Amanda smiled. "I'm more than alright, Mom."

"Thank God. I was so scared, honey."

"I was safe the whole time. Really, I was." Perhaps it was the discussion she'd had with Jordan about the parents they had both lost, or perhaps it was the tension of the storm finally easing, but Amanda was desperate to reassure her mother. "I was warm, and safe, and out of harm's way."

"Your apartment made it through, then?"

"No. I didn't stay at my apartment."

Amanda heard her mother's pause, felt the confusion through the phone line. "You stayed in a shelter?"

"No, Mom. With a friend."

Friend. Amanda mused over that word while her mother talked to her about what the storm had been like and what they had seen on the evening news. It felt odd to call Jordan her friend. A week ago she would have called him her teacher, but now even the word friend didn't seem to make much sense.

"You and your friend, where did you stay?"

The question shook Amanda back into the present. "In a house away from town. It was scary sometimes, but the damage was really almost nothing. It just took a day to fix. We were lucky."

The silence stretched out, and suddenly Amanda knew what her mother would say. She beat her to the punch, the words surprising Amanda just as much as they surprised her mother. "I stayed at my boyfriend's house, Mom."

"Your boyfriend?"

"Yeah."

Much to Amanda's surprise, her mother laughed out loud. "Good for you, honey."

Good for you?

"Mom? What's wrong with you?"

Her mother's smile came loud and clear through the phone line. "I'm glad you have someone to take care of you, honey. I should have known you would have told me about the man when the time was right. I knew you didn't move out of the house to be on your own. I just knew it!"

Amanda shook her head in disbelief. Why was it so hard for her mother to believe she had really wanted to make it on her own? Did everything have to have an ulterior motive?

"I have to go, Mom."

Amanda's mother heard the anger in her voice and tried to soothe things over. "Honey, should we talk about this?"

"I'm helping out at the shelter, and I really have to go. I'll call again soon."

She hung up the phone and stared at it for a long moment, listening to the sounds of the makeshift shelter just outside the door. Amanda was rattled by her mother's ability to completely deny all the things she had said over the last several months. Had her mother simply waited for an explanation that suited the way she wanted the world to be, instead of recognizing her daughter for the adult she was, who was capable of making adult decisions?

Amanda closed her eyes and took a deep breath. She would go back to that apartment and salvage her things, and then she would find another place, maybe one closer to the school, so she wouldn't have to drive, and she could save more money …

Then Amanda remembered Jordan. She would need a place to stay until she could find somewhere permanent, and he was going to offer. She had already heard the words that he stopped himself from uttering—she saw them in his eyes when he looked at her. But staying with him, even for a few days, was a dangerous thing, and she knew it. It would be easy to get too comfortable, to enjoy him too much, and then come to rely on him. If she wanted to make it on her own, to prove she could do it, she certainly didn't need to become dependent on a man.

Amanda wiped the tears from her eyes, straightened her shoulders, and opened the door to the sounds of hustle and bustle. She was here to help, and that's what she would do. She would figure out the rest later.

Chapter Eight

Jordan watched Amanda as she moved through the remains of her apartment, picking up small things that had survived the storm and putting them in a cardboard box. Jordan was standing beside the armoire, pulling out clothes that were more or less alright. A few spins in the washing machine and most of Amanda's clothes would be good as new.

He watched as she knelt down to reach under the bed. She came up with a small wooden box, opened it carefully, and smiled broadly when she saw the papers inside were virtually untouched. She tucked the box between some of her other belongings and walked gingerly to the bathroom, glass crunching under her feet. She peeked in for a moment, then backed away. She caught Jordan looking at her.

"There's nothing in the bathroom I need," she said.

"Most of your clothes look good," he said. "You might lose a few pieces, but not many."

This was the second day they had ventured into town. Amanda had been too tired after a long day of working in the shelter to protest when Jordan urged her into the truck and drove them both back to his house. They were surprised to come around the corner and see the lights on, repaired sometime while they were in town.

She had trudged up the stairs, almost fallen asleep in the shower, and then crawled between sheets that were warm and blessedly dry. She didn't remember falling asleep, and she knew Jordan had let her sleep in way past the time they should have gone back to the school. She awoke to the smell of bacon and eggs—and a stomach that was growling for food.

He had smiled at her while standing in front of the stove, spatula in hand, and she had felt familiar light of happiness.

Now he was helping her go through her things, but she hadn't yet breached the subject of where she would stay, or when she would find another apartment.

"Jordan?"

He dropped a sweater into the box and smiled at her.

"I've been thinking about what I'm going to do. I'm going to have to find another apartment soon."

Jordan nodded and suddenly couldn't seem to meet her eyes. "I figured you would want to."

"Are you upset about that?"

He uttered a small laugh. "I shouldn't be. I know you had a place of your own, and a life of your own, and the hurricane shouldn't change that. I also know it's a bad idea for you to simply move into my house, for a variety of reasons."

"It's awkward," she admitted. "I'm so comfortable with you, and after this week, I feel as though I've known you forever. Moving into a new place of my own feels ..."

"I know."

She slipped close to him, looked around to see if anyone might be watching, and kissed him gently. He returned her affection in kind, running his hands up her back, pulling her tighter against him, not giving a damn who might see.

"The college would fire you if I moved in," she murmured against his lips.

He chuckled. "I could be fired for kissing you right now."

Though they both knew it was true, neither of them moved away.

"How is this going to work, Jordan? I can't simply walk into a classroom and see you behind the podium and think of you as my teacher. I know you are, but ... you're not."

"I don't know how I can treat you like just another student."

"I don't want you to."

The sounds of a car approaching from a side street made them slowly pull apart. Amanda looked at him from over the armoire as she picked up her cardboard box of belongings. "I think we're almost done. It's a good thing I didn't have much to lose, huh?"

He finished cleaning out the armoire and gently closed it. The door bulged in the frame, warped by the water and wind. He gently pushed the remnants of a chandelier with the toe of his boot. "It's not that you had little to lose. I think it's that you know what matters, and none of this material stuff matters."

"But it's funny," she mused. "I was so scared of what the storm would do to your house."

"Maybe it wasn't the house you were worried about, so much as the history of it."

Amanda smiled and lifted her face to the sunlight. Even after such a short time, Jordan knew her so well. He could almost always finish her thoughts. They could communicate with just a look. It was the kind of comfort she had seen before in other people, and had hoped she would find one day. She just hadn't expected to find it so soon, or in such an unlikely place.

"Where do you want to go?"

She shrugged at the question. "I was thinking about a place closer to the college."

"No, silly. Where do you want to go today?"

Amanda laughed and shook her head. "My mind is all over the place these days. I'm scattered."

"You're not the only one," he whispered from behind her, dropping a kiss on the side of her neck before he moved toward the ladder.

"Is there anything we need to do in your office?"

He carefully swung down on the ladder, went down a few rungs, and carefully picked up the box. He balanced it against the ladder and let it slide down as he took each step. "No. The Dean let me know it was all cleaned up already—the maintenance crew did it."

"Wow."

"That's what I said. If they did mine, they did all the others in the building, too. That's a lot of work. Anyway, we don't have to go to the campus. So where do you want to go?"

They decided to get out of town. They were both tired of hiding their affection for each other, for fear of someone from the college seeing that they were much more than just teacher and student. Jordan expressed doubts that his old truck would make it that far, but Amanda reminded him that they had just come through a hurricane—what was a little breakdown in the slow lane? Jordan laughed, put his hand on her thigh, and pointed the old truck toward the interstate.

They wound up in Amish country, a small community that appeared to have come through the hurricane unscathed. They drove the gravel and dirt roads at a crawl, watching the horses and farmers and the occasional woman in a long dress and bonnet as she hung clean clothes on the line. They wandered into a small shop, admired the hand-made toys and quilts and furniture, then had a piece of bread that melted in their mouths. The milk was fresh, rich with cream. The young lady behind the counter blushed at their compliments and smiled shyly as Jordan purchased more than a few of her homemade jams.

"You could live this way," Amanda said to him as they passed a buggy. The horse ignored them. The man behind the reins waved.

Jordan smiled, remembering. "Where I lived in Tennessee, there were several Amish communities within a quick drive. I would go down there, park on the side of the road, and just walk. Just breathe. Even the air was different there, like the absence of electricity and cars and all the modern conveniences had returned the world to the way it was meant to be.

"The people there were always so welcoming. They never asked why some guy was out there walking around on their roads. When they asked how my day was going, it wasn't a quick question. They really cared to hear the answer, and they waited until they got it."

"They paid attention. That's rare, isn't it?"

Jordan turned onto another road. They watched a boy riding a contraption across the field. The machine was pulled by an enormous horse. The animal pulled the weight as if it was nothing. Jordan rolled down the window and they were quiet, just listening to the jingle of the harness and the occasional calls of the boy, who talked to the horse in an accent they didn't recognize.

"I think it comes from being in a world that doesn't move so fast. It's all about family, home, making a living from the land, honoring the beliefs that have been passed on through countless generations. That kind of mentality is dying. It used to be that those who were different from the Amish were the ones who were considered odd. Now it's the other way around."

"I don't like the way the world is sometimes," she admitted. "The rules always change. The expectations are always so high, and for things that don't matter anyway. It's hard to know what is right and what is wrong."

Jordan was silent for a long time, making Amanda wonder if he had heard what she said. When he finally did speak, it wasn't at all what she expected. "This is killing you, isn't it?"

"What?" she asked, confused.

"What did your mother say to you?" he countered. "Ever since you talked to her, you've been philosophical one minute, closed off the next. What did she say?"

Amanda picked at a torn part of the seat cover, refusing to look him in the eye. "She said she just knew I had moved out of her house for a man. She had just been waiting for me to tell her."

"That's not what happened, is it?"

"No." Amanda sighed and threw up her hands in frustration. "What does she want? The world to be her own little way, with no deviation from it? Why can't she see I really am a woman with my own mind, my own wants, and the ability to make my own choices that have nothing to do with anyone else?"

Jordan said nothing as Amanda went on. She needed to get the words out, but beyond that, Jordan wasn't sure of what to say. His desire to have Amanda in his house all the time, his desire to make things work between them, was at odds with the things Amanda was determined to do.

Jordan knew better than to tie anyone down—he knew that ended in failure. He had to be careful not to move too fast, not to make the mistake of jumping into a relationship because he was lonely. He needed to put on the brakes, keep that door open for Amanda, and in the meantime, help her do whatever she needed to do.

Though he was trying to be logical about the whole thing, it still hurt like hell.

"Jordan? What are you thinking?"

He looked at her, almost lost in his own thoughts. "There are some good apartments near the college, on Stewart Street. We can look at those tomorrow morning, if you want. School won't start again until Monday, and by then you will have some sense of where you're going to land."

Amanda nodded slowly, stung by his quick agreement that she should move into a place of her own as soon as possible. Why was she so upset he was agreeing with her?

"There are some good apartments on Seaboard, too."

They looked at each other, neither of them knowing what to say, both of them sorry to feel the tension in the truck. Jordan ended the discussion by putting the truck into drive and moving along the road, leaving the boy and his plowhorse behind.

"Let's enjoy ourselves today," he said.

•

They stopped for dinner at a little café just outside of town, a place neither of them had ever been. The waitress gave them a table in the very back, where they talked over the menus in hushed voices, happy to be anonymous, certain this might be one of the last times they would have the chance.

"When classes are back in session next week," he said, "are you going to be there?"

"Of course. I might be dating the teacher, but I still have to worry about my attendance."

She winked at him, and Jordan laughed out loud. He reached over the salt shakers and took her hand. "We'll have to make this work, Amanda. I still want to see you, spend time with you. I want to see where this goes."

"So how will it work? You will have to treat me like anyone else."

Jordan ran his fingers through his hair, frustrated already. "Hell, I don't know. I understand why the fraternization rules are in place. I get it, I really do. But that doesn't mean I like it right now."

"Have you ever dated a student before?" The question was casual, but the emotion behind it was not. It mattered to Amanda to know the answer.

"No. Never even considered it."

"Would you have considered it if we weren't trapped in that house together?"

"No," he said. "I know that sounds bad, considering where we are now. But at the time, I was so serious about following the rules, I never would have looked at you that way."

"Not even that day in the parking lot?"

Jordan smiled, remembering. "Not even then. What about you?"

She took a sip of her soda. "I thought you were a stud."

Jordan almost choked on his water, drawing the attention of several tables. When he calmed down, he chuckled at her, blushing all the while. "A stud?"

She gave him a wicked grin. "I was right."

Their dinners arrived, and Jordan watched her while they ate. She was so far beyond her years, so much more mature than he had been at her age. He never would have been able to handle the kind of relationship they were discussing. He had a newfound respect for her strength and determination, and he was glad to have the chance to help her.

"We'll find you an apartment tomorrow," he said. "But tonight, will you stay with me?"

She smiled and fed him a piece of chicken. She didn't have to answer.

Chapter Nine

The first day back to school went quite smoothly, despite the chaos the faculty expected. Classrooms had been moved temporarily to allow for repairs, but students seemed to find their way without much of a problem.

The dorm rooms were another matter—students were sleeping on the floors in some cases, while they waited for the damage to be remedied. The campus had the manpower and the resources, but simply hadn't had enough time to get to all of the buildings yet.

Advanced English Composition was moved out of the Frost Building and into Draker, the tall building across the quad. Jordan was instantly envious of the classroom—it had a full view of the quad from one side, and a gorgeous view of a church steeple from the other. The chalkboards were newer than his, too. He made a mental note to hit up the Dean for some of those once the repairs were finished and the school was back to normal.

When Amanda walked into the classroom with her backpack on her shoulder and a secret smile on her lips, it was all Jordan could do to keep from staring. In the days since she had found a new apartment, they hadn't seen much of each other. The first time Jordan went back to his house alone, he was greeted with a silence that was more oppressive than any he'd ever felt. He had become accustomed to being alone, and so it hadn't bothered him—now that he knew what it was like to be with someone again, he wanted that all the time. Silence didn't suit him at all.

Callie missed Amanda, too. She sniffed around his feet when he came in, then ran to the door to look for the other person she expected. When she realized Amanda wasn't out there, she climbed behind the couch and sulked. Only a fresh can of tuna could coax her out of her hiding place. She glared at Jordan, as if it was his fault that Amanda wasn't there.

Now Jordan watched the students file in, greeting each one in turn, but his eyes kept drifting to Amanda. She set her backpack on the floor, drew out a notebook and pencil, then shot him a quiet grin before turning to talk to one of her classmates.

The lesson went well, and for a brief while, Jordan managed to forget his girlfriend was sitting right there in the second row. He concentrated on the lecture, watched for who was taking notes and who wasn't, and called questions out to those few students who seemed to be paying more attention to their own thoughts than to what he was trying to teach them.

He gave the assignment, listened to the obligatory groans, and turned to write notes on the board for his next class. He listened to the chairs pushing back, the backpacks zipping, and the footsteps out the door.

He knew Amanda was still there. He wrote on the board as she came up behind him, and after a moment, her hand touched his back.

"You looked so sexy up there," she murmured.

The chalk broke in his hand. He grinned as he picked up one of the pieces and started to write again. "Do you have any idea what you do to me?"

"You can show me later."

This was a new Amanda, bolder than he had known her to be. He turned to look at her. Her eyes sparkled with mischief. "Are you trying to get me in trouble, Miss Whitmore?"

"You're already in trouble, Dr. Eversole."

If that wasn't the truth, Jordan didn't know what was. He turned back to the board, but not before reaching out to squeeze her hand. He let go just as the first student for his next class came through the door. Amanda walked away without a word, but Jordan knew she was smiling.

The school day dragged on, longer than any Jordan could remember. Once he sneaked into his office during a break and pulled out Amanda's file. Her class schedule was in there, and he felt like he was sneaking a look at something he had no right to see, even though the file had come from his own cabinet. He glanced over her transcripts and paid close attention to one of her essays. Why had he filed it in there? He couldn't remember, but this time when he read over it, he savored every last word.

"You're obsessed," he said to himself as he put the file back in its proper place. "You are obsessed with a girl young enough to be your daughter."

Jordan found it amazing he really didn't care about the age difference. In fact, it had hardly crossed his mind at all. Amanda had proven that age was really just a number. Sometimes, Jordan thought she was much more mature than he was.

He went back to his temporary classroom with a smile that stayed in place for the rest of the day.

That afternoon, he put his briefcase into the truck and cursed the fact that his car was going to be in the shop for a long, long time. There were dozens of cars that were priorities, far more important than his, and he would have to wait his turn. He missed the wind in his hair and the power of the engine under his hands.

Amanda caught him just as he was putting the truck into drive. He paused and let her approach him, very aware that faculty and staff were everywhere, not to mention the hundreds of students going back to their dorms after classes. She stood a safe distance from the truck, smiled sweetly, and spoke to him as she would speak to any other professor on campus.

"Good afternoon, Dr. Eversole. Did you have a good day?"

He grinned, knowing full well what she was doing. His whole day had been spent thinking about her, and she knew it. "It was a fine day, Amanda. How about you?"

"Filled with daydreams," she admitted.

"I know how that feels."

She looked around her and waved to someone on the sidewalk. "I wanted to tell you to have a good night. I have a lot of studying to get done, and I have to work at the store tonight."

"I might have to go to the store later."

They longed to touch each other, but kept their distance. He revved the engine, making a show of impatience, but the reality was that he could have sat there all day and just looked at her. She backed slowly away from the truck, never breaking eye contact, and suddenly he swung around and put her backpack on her shoulder, walking off in the direction of her new apartment, never looking back. Jordan watched her go.

The way she ran her fingers through her hair, pushing it back from her forehead, kept his attention. He liked the way she walked, the way she waved, the way she laughed at someone's comment at the crosswalk. He liked watching her.

Out of nowhere, the thought came, and it made his heart pound in his chest.

I could fall in love with her.

•

Back at her apartment, Amanda threw down her books and looked over the empty space. This apartment was furnished quite like the old one, with only the bare necessities. Miss Ellie had come through the storm just fine, and had taken the destruction of her house with the attitude of someone who had a great deal of insurance. She had given Amanda her deposit, her month's worth of rent and then some extra, despite Amanda's arguments.

"You will take that money, child. And I won't hear another word of it."

"Miss Ellie," she had started, and the old woman cut her off with a glare.

"You listen to me, young lady. I've watched you work hard, and study hard, and you've made it all on your own, without anybody to help you. That's impressive at any age. Now you've been through a hurricane, and you've lost everything you had, and I'm willing to bet you didn't have much money put away. Some, because you're that kind of girl, but not much. Am I right?"

Amanda blushed, and that was all the answer Miss Ellie needed.

"So you take this. I'm going to be getting insurance money, more than I need, and you deserve something for everything you lost. You should know by now that arguing with me won't work, so you will take that money. Put it in the bank and don't use it if you want, but either way, make an old lady happy. I don't want to worry about you, girl."

In the face of such a request, Amanda couldn't argue. "Okay, Miss Ellie. Thank you."

"You're welcome. Now, where are you going?"

"I found an apartment over on the other side of town. It's close to the college, so I don't have to drive. It's going to take a while before I can save up for another car."

"You didn't have insurance?"

Amanda cringed. "Liability only."

Miss Ellie pinned her with a look that spoke volumes. "You don't need a lecture, do you? From now on, you'll have full coverage."

"Yes."

Amanda had put the money in the bank, used it for the deposit on the new apartment, and now she was thinking about buying something nice for it. Something like a candle, maybe, or a pretty picture frame. Maybe she could put a picture of her mother in it. She hadn't called her since that day at the shelter, and she felt guilty for not picking up the phone, but she wasn't sure she could control her anger, either. She might say things she didn't mean—or worse, things she did mean—and that would do more harm than good.

Amanda opened her freezer and pulled out a frozen dinner. It was the best she could do under the circumstances, but she got paid tomorrow, and that would be a good thing. Thankfully, the store hadn't been damaged beyond easy repair, and she still had a job.

She put the dinner in the oven and sat down at the kitchen table. The chair creaked under her, but the table was sturdy. She opened her science textbook and her notebook, then looked at notes for several minutes, yet didn't remember a single thing. All she could think about was that big house in the middle of nowhere, Callie the cat, and Jordan.

What was he doing? What was he working on? She knew he wouldn't attack the paperwork for class first—she knew he would be busy working on something for the house. What was it?

She finally laid her head down on her science book, wished she could call him, then realized she didn't have a phone yet. She missed him terribly, and she had just seen him an hour ago.

This was going to be a long, long night.

•

Jordan drove to the far side of town and picked up a load of lumber. He tucked supplies into the the passenger seat, and set buckets of paint on the floorboard. The old truck was running well, and as long as he had no choice but to drive it everywhere, he might as well put it to good use. At this rate, he would have enough supplies and lumber to last throughout the winter and far beyond.

By the time he finished loading the lumber and picking out the paint for the bedrooms upstairs, the sun was going down. The town looked better after a week's worth of repairs, but there were still far too many homes with roofs gone, open to the elements while the owners waited on the inevitable red-tape of the insurance companies.

Jordan drove slowly through the streets, looking at the progress. His truck seemed to drive of its own accord to the department store, where he parked under the bright lights of the neon sign and looked through the plate-glass window.

He couldn't see Amanda in there, but he knew she was working—she had told him so more than once, as if inviting him to come visit her whenever the mood struck. He touched the steering wheel as he watched the people move around inside. He did need things from the store, but what, he couldn't remember. He knew he wanted to see her.

Jordan climbed out of the truck and was met by one of his fellow teachers as she came out of the sliding doors. She smiled at him. "Fancy seeing you here," she said. "Want to help me lug some of this stuff to the car?"

Jordan obliged, bantering and talking all the way, but inside he was worried. Anyone could run into him here. Anyone might see him hovering a bit too much, or talking a bit too long to the pretty brunette in there, the one who just so happened to be his student. As he waved the teacher off and watched the taillights blink at the corner light, Jordan started to get angry.

Why do I have to hide anything?

He turned on his heel and walked into the store, the sliding doors whooshing open in front of him. Just as quickly as he had been determined to make his feelings known, he lost his nerve when he saw the dozens of people walking the aisles. He instead walked casually through the store, looking here and there with a nonchalant air, hoping to see Amanda on every new aisle.

He found her at the pharmacy.

She didn't look up as he approached. She was dressed in the uniform of the store, a surprisingly flattering polo shirt and matching slacks. In her hand was something that looked like a radar gun. She consulted the screen, ran the flashing red line over the UPC of the product in front of her, listened to the beep, and then went to the next one.

Jordan stepped into an aisle of housewares and watched her from around the end of it. He liked the way her hair swayed in the ponytail. He even liked the way she stretched, putting her hand to her back as it if hurt.

"Need a massage?" he asked quietly, coming up behind her. She whipped around to look at him. He watched the expression in her wide eyes change from surprise to happy recognition.

"From you?" she whispered to him, looking down at the UPCs and smiling.

"Who else?"

They stood quietly, with a few feet between them, as a woman walked down the pharmacy aisle. Jordan pretended to be very interested in the thermometers. Amanda simply went about her work, doing a fine job of ignoring him while he studied her out of the corner of his eye. As soon as the shopper turned the corner, Jordan reached out and touched the back of Amanda's hand with his fingertips. She shot him a quick smile.

"I'm glad you came by," she said. "I've missed you."

"It's only been a few hours."

"Don't remind me," she groaned, scanning another UPC. "I was missing you an hour after you left."

"It took you that long?"

Amanda laughed and smiled openly at him, throwing caution to the wind. She took her time enjoying the view, the way his hair curled just-so over his ears, the light of mischief in his eyes. They looked at each other until the uneven squeak of a shopping cart said another customer was approaching. Jordan touched her hand once more and turned the corner, working his way down the aisles, coming back once more just to glance at her, and then paying for his purchases and leaving the store.

He turned up the radio and sang along all the way home. Once there, he fed Callie and unloaded the lumber, making a nice stack on the front porch. He took the paint upstairs, and even though it was getting late, he popped open a bucket and dipped in a brush. The yellow paint looked fantastic when he was done with one small piece of trim. Now that the house had made it through a hurricane, he felt as though it was invincible, and he couldn't wait to turn it into a showplace. He was tired of living in a construction zone.

Jordan cleaned the brush in the sink, whistling. When he looked up into the mirror, he was smiling.

•

Amanda walked home in a fog of happiness. Jordan had come to see her at the store! The simple fact he had hung around, peeking at her when he thought she wasn't looking, meant she was walking on clouds by the time her shift was finished. She helped lock up and hit the road, not thinking about homework or bills or anything but the man she couldn't wait to see again.

She was standing under a streetlight, waiting for the crosswalk sign to change, when the reality of what she was doing hit her like a ton of bricks. The thought came out of nowhere, and later she thought about that moment and realized all of life was that way—the most important parts of it happened in an instant, without much thought.

I could fall in love with him.

She crossed the street, watching either way for cars, the words echoing in her head. From the outside she looked different, she was sure. She would have to look different, wouldn't she? After all, she wasn't the same person she had been a month ago, or even a week ago. She had dealt with so many changes in that time, some good and some decidedly bad, but each one of them had flavored the way she tasted the world. The woman she used to be would never return, and Amanda was sure this was only a good thing.

Love. Falling in love would change someone for the better. It would have to be for the better, for it was something that opened the very soul, made a person more vulnerable, more open, and more generous. There would be some difference in her—some look in her eyes, a blush to her cheeks, a smile on her lips that was just a little bit different than it had been before.

She thought about Jordan, about the things she noticed now. She had thought the way he smiled, the jokes he cracked, the light in his eyes, were all things that she simply hadn't noticed before. For the first time, she wondered if the changes were there because he was falling in love, too.

Amanda, ever the rational and realistic young woman, threw her arms into the air and let out a whoop of joy.

Chapter Ten

The days ran together, one into another. The tone of those first days set the tone for the ones that followed. Amanda and Jordan spent as much time together as they could without drawing attention to themselves. On her nights off, she sometimes walked down to the marsh and met him there, where their odds of running into anyone they knew were pretty low, and then took his truck back to the big house in the middle of nowhere.

There they would give in to the things they wanted to do all week, but couldn't. It was sheer joy for Jordan to simply hold Amanda in his arms and kiss her, as though he was a teenager again and kissing his girlfriend was his favorite pastime. Amanda reveled in holding his hand as they walked through the fields, looking at the land around them, listening to Jordan's plans for it. They worked hard—painting walls and hammering nails, slowly breathing life back into the house that had been vacant for so many years.

As those long evenings became cooler, they stayed in the house, watching each other by candlelight over a dinner Amanda had cooked, or watching a movie on the sofa while they cuddled together in the light of the screen. When they were too sleepy to watch anymore, they climbed the creaking staircase to the master bedroom and crawled under the warm sheets.

Even when she wasn't there, Amanda's presence was clear in the house. Her alarm clock graced the bedside table, along with some of her jewelry and a tube of lipstick. Downstairs, the fresh flowers on the table were her handiwork, and her favorite sodas were in the fridge.

The stronger their relationship became, the harder it was to keep the rest of the world from discovering it. It took a great deal of effort for Jordan to treat her like anyone else on campus, and it took effort for Amanda to treat him like a teacher. Jordan found himself wondering if he was doing the right things, or if he was drawing more attention to them. Was he calling on her in class a little too often? Or was he ignoring her a little too much? Was he seen talking to her too often in the halls, laughing a little too loudly, caressing her with his eyes a little inappropriately?

Amanda wondered the same things. That's why she stayed away from his office when she could have sneaked in, and why she hesitated to stay after class, though she wanted to simply hear his voice when it dropped a bit lower, quieter, words meant only for her. She said nothing of him to her friends, but much to her surprise, she opened up to her mother.

"He wants to have Thanksgiving at his house, Mom," Amanda said one night in October, when she and her mother were having a civil, if not entirely friendly, conversation. The tension was still there, but it had dissipated substantially since August. "I wondered if you would come?"

There was a moment of silence, and then her mother said what Amanda knew she would say. "What about dinner here? We always invite Aunt Marilyn. That's what we do."

"We could do both," she answered immediately, having thought for many hours about how she would handle this expected and justified complaint.

"Yes, we could," her mother said, surprising Amanda almost into speechlessness. When she hung up the phone, the nerves began. She called Jordan to tell him the news.

"She doesn't know about the age difference," Amanda admitted. "She doesn't even know you are faculty at the school. I haven't known how to tell her, or even if I should."

"Maybe I can win her over," he said with a grin, and Amanda laughed out loud. Of course he could win her over. Hadn't he done the same thing to her?

Thanksgiving Day dawned crisp and clear. The house smelled of turkey, dressing and sweet potatoes as Jordan came down the staircase. Amanda had been up for hours, making a dinner that would make any southern cook proud. She smiled at him as he rubbed his eyes, stirring something in a pot with one hand and reaching out to him with the other. "Come here and kiss me."

Jordan did just that, and stayed there long enough that whatever was in the pot began to smell suspiciously smoky. With a yelp she moved away from him and turned down the heat, then peered into the pot with a critical eye. "I think it's okay."

"What is it?"

"Broccoli casserole. Or at least, it will be."

Jordan winced and looked over her shoulder. There was broccoli in that pot, alright. He was sure this was the first time a stalk of broccoli had been in his house. "I hate broccoli."

She grinned as she turned the pot upside down over the strainer. "I don't."

"Good. You can have my share."

She pecked him on the cheek as they heard a car coming up the driveway. Her mother wasn't expected for another two hours or so. "Who could that be?" he asked, even as he walked toward the front door.

The woman who stepped into the house was tall, lithe and gorgeous. Amanda brushed a wayward strand of hair from her eyes as the brunette caught sight of her, stopped to stare for a moment, then turned to Jordan. She was whispering, almost hissing, and from the way she was gesturing in the air, it was obvious the woman was angry.

Amanda dropped the pot holder on the counter, watching. The woman turned in her direction, pointed at her, and went on with whatever tirade she was in the middle of delivering. Amanda stepped around the counter and came toward them. Callie jumped up on the couch and kneaded the fabric nervously, watching the couple as the argument grew more heated.

"Katie, that's enough!" Jordan finally exploded, and the words stopped Amanda dead in her tracks.

Katie. His ex-wife.

Katie shut her mouth. She took a step back, glared at Jordan, and then turned to look at Amanda. Through the space of a dozen heartbeats, the two women studied each other. Amanda had heard the story of how Jordan's marriage had begun and how it had ended, and she had heard a few small details about Katie. She was a counselor in a high school. She was brunette, very tall. She came from money and never let Jordan forget it. She was getting remarried.

What else was there? As Amanda remembered the things Jordan had said, Katie pinned her with a withering glare. Her question was blunt and entirely inappropriate.

"How old are you?"

Amanda's eyes widened in surprise. She wasn't sure what she expected to hear, but it certainly wasn't this! The need for a level head was foremost in her mind, so she calmly answered, "My name is Amanda."

"She can't even answer a simple question," Katie railed, looking back at Jordan. "Is she even a college student? You usually teach them better than that."

Amanda, shocked at the bravery of the woman in front of her, was speechless. The look on Jordan's face was dark, dangerous, something she had never seen before. He was holding his tongue, but clearly it wasn't because he didn't know what to say.

Amanda listened to a few more snide remarks before she found her voice. "Excuse me."

Katie whirled around, her eyes filled with anger—and something else. Something that surprised Amanda and made her back down just the slightest bit.

Katie was hurt.

They stared at each other, the space between then crackling with tension.

"My name is Amanda," she began again. "Jordan and I were just in the kitchen, cooking. Was there a reason you came out here today? If there is, we would both appreciate it if you would get on with it, and then let us get on with the rest of our day."

Katie glared at her. "We?"

"Yes. We would appreciate it if you would get to your reasons for being here."

The older woman sniffed and raised her nose in the air, as if smelling something distasteful. "Alright. I came out here to see for myself. I had heard Jordan was moving on, which is fine and dandy with me, but then I heard he was moving on with a woman much younger than himself, and quite possibly a student—both of which, as I'm sure you know, are at best not a good idea, and at worst, possibly a breach of the college rules."

Amanda nodded. "You mean, a woman younger than you?"

Katie took a step toward Amanda, and suddenly Jordan moved. He grabbed Katie's shoulder and spun her around to face him instead. "You will not," he said.

"She's a disrespectful little whelp," Katie proclaimed. "She's trying to deliberately pick a fight here. She's not seeing the big picture."

Jordan shook his head. Much to Amanda's surprise and Katie's fury, he smiled. "The big picture is so clear, it could be projected on a movie screen. You just got remarried, didn't you? But you're out here at your ex-husband's house, on Thanksgiving Day of all times, whining about the woman he's dating now, when you have no reason whatsoever to care. In fact, you have no reason to ever darken my door again. I wonder why you're here, Katie? Why you're really here."

Katie dropped all the defenses. Amanda saw them go, saw the slack in her posture, saw the change in her face. Katie no longer looked regal and young. Instead, she looked bitter and much older than her years. "I'm here because I hate you, Jordan Eversole, and I will ruin you if it is the last thing I do!"

The screeching threat silenced everyone. The house was so quiet, they could all hear the bubbling of the broccoli on the stove and the tiny meow from Callie, who was watching the whole scene from her spot on the couch.

Jordan reached behind him and opened the door. It hit the wall with a force that shook the whole house. Katie flinched, on the verge of tears, as Jordan pointed to the porch and ordered, "Get out of my house."

When Katie hesitated, Jordan leaned toward her. "Get out right now."

Amanda watched as Katie walked out of the house, her head held as high as she could make it, her arms wrapped around her as if she were freezing. She walked down the steps slowly, approached her car, stopped halfway, then reconsidered and kept going. Amanda came to the front door just as Katie was driving out of the yard, kicking up the late-summer dust with her tires, even though she was moving at a crawl. They watched her go and then stood in silence, staring at the place where she had been.

"She's still in love with you," Amanda said.

"She's going to make life a living hell."

Amanda looked up at the tears in Jordan's eyes. He wrapped his arms around her and kissed the top of her head. Amanda clung to him, even though the broccoli was probably burning and the biscuits needed cutting and the time was getting short. She held onto him while he fought to get his emotions under control.

"I'm happy," he finally said. "I'm happy with you. It's been a long time since I was happy. Why can't she let me have that?"

Amanda had no answers. She just held onto him until he was ready to let go.

•

The broccoli was ruined. Amanda threw it out the back door, where a squirrel immediately came to inspect it. He nibbled a bit and then scampered up a tree.

"Even the squirrel can't stand the smell," Amanda teased, trying to get Jordan out of the dark mood he had been in ever since Katie had walked through the door. Jordan wordlessly took the pan and rinsed it out in the sink.

"I'm sorry we won't have broccoli casserole today," he said.

Amanda started mixing up a pie crust. She thought about her grandmother, who had taught her everything she knew about working in a kitchen. She had dispensed just as much wisdom as recipes. What would the wise old woman think about her relationship with Jordan?

"We'll have more than enough food. Nobody will miss the broccoli."

Jordan watched her roll out the crust. She slipped it into the pan and fluted the edges with experienced fingertips. She sliced strawberries and dropped them in, tasting more than a few before they got to the pie, then she sliced the rhubarb. Jordan studied her every movement, thinking about how Katie never cooked anything homemade, how she was far too modern for that.

It seemed Katie would be the first one to turn the other way when she saw a sizable age difference between two lovers, but apparently her modern ways had their limits.

Amanda rolled out another crust, and this time she sliced it to make a lattice top. Jordan smiled at the way the pie turned out. It looked like a professional job. Amanda slid it into the oven, stood back to admire her work, then closed the door and reached for another mixing bowl.

"Come here," Jordan murmured, tired of watching and not touching.

She looked at him from across the counter as she picked up a potato and started to peel it. "I'm alright, Jordan. I recognize what happened this morning for what it was. Your ex-wife is upset you're moving on, and besides that, you're moving on with someone younger than she is. Most women might not care, but she strikes me as the kind of woman who cares about appearances and what others think."

"She's going to go to the Dean," he said, looking at Amanda with misty eyes. "She's not going to let this go."

Amanda sliced the potato into quarters. She filled a pot with water and set it on the stove, listening to the hiss of the flame under it. While the water heated to boiling, she went back to the potatoes. "We knew this kind of thing could happen," she said.

"What are we going to do?"

Amanda shook her head. "I don't know," she said. "We're going to wing it, I guess."

Jordan put his head down on the counter and groaned. "I wish I could hate her."

"You're not that kind of man."

Amanda sliced another potato into quarters. The water now had small bubbles on the top, but it still wasn't boiling hard enough. Amanda watched the water move as she thought about how things would be. "I could transfer to another school."

Jordan's voice was harsh. "No."

"If she does go to the Dean, the nature of our relationship is not going to matter. It will be considered inappropriate, and no amount of talking will make it look any better. It will have to end, or I will have to stop being a student. It's that simple."

Jordan turned to look out the window. The leaves were

falling fast, making a carpet of gold across the yard. He hadn't bothered to rake them up, enjoying the colors for as long as he could before the winter took over. How many times had he and Amanda sat on the porch swing and watched them fall? How often had she kicked through them on an autumn night, making him smile with her natural, unaffected manner?

There had to be an answer. He just had to find it.

"You're grasping at straws," she said, reading his mind. She dropped the potatoes in the water. The boiling stopped for a moment, then started up again, harder than before. She sprinkled in salt and pepper, and then started snipping chives on the cutting board. She pulled out the whipping cream.

"I can figure this out," he said.

Amanda put the knife down on the board and pinned him with a glare that was almost as white-hot as Katie's had been. "Stop this. Stop it right now. You're a big boy, Jordan, and you know what we're into here. You knew it from day one, what it might do to your career, or to my schooling, or to our relationship. There is no way out of this. There are only ways around it, and those are the things you should be focusing on."

Jordan stared at her, aware again of how mature she really was, relieved that she had taken the lead and said it like it was—even if she had put him in his place by doing so.

"I love you," he said.

Amanda's eyes widened. Her mouth fell open. Her hands began to shake. Jordan watched the shock race over her features, then he watched the realization and the calm acceptance take its place. The smile she gave him as radiant, full of life and promise.

"I love you, too," she said.

•

An hour later, Jordan stood on the porch and said hello to Amanda's mother.

"I'm Jordan," he said, extending his hand to her.

She looked up at him with wide eyes, so much like Amanda's, and shook his hand. "I'm Anna."

"It's so good to meet you," he said. "I've looked forward to this for months."

She suddenly smiled. "You're so handsome!"

"Mother!" Amanda was standing at the door, her voice stern, but on her face was a smile.

Anna waggled a finger at Amanda, grinning. "Seems there are many things you haven't told me about, young lady." She cast a skeptical eye at Jordan. "How old are you?"

The question, coming from Anna and laced with an air of teasing, was entirely different from the angry question thrown out by Katie that very morning. Jordan grinned and gave it right back to her, raising an eyebrow and admitting, "Old enough to be her daddy."

Anna gave him a saucy wink. Jordan liked her immediately.

Amanda opened the door and her mother stepped past Jordan to embrace her. Jordan stood back, watching with a smile on his face, while the two women greeted each other after the long months of misunderstandings. Both of them dissolved into tears and then into laughter, making Jordan wonder how women did such things—they seemed to have the market cornered on crying and laughing all at the same time.

"We burned the broccoli," Amanda said, and her mother sniffled.

"It's just as well. I always hated the stuff."

Amanda looked at her mother in surprise. "But you made it every year!"

Anna nodded. "Your father loved it. You ate it because you wanted to be like him, and after he was gone I just kept making it for you."

Amanda hugged her mother again. "I kept asking for it because I thought you liked it." Her laugh was shaky. "I think we need to work on communication, don't you?"

"You did make the good mashed potatoes, right? The ones Auntie likes?"

"Of course I did." Amanda, overcome by affection, kissed her mother on the cheek. "Where is Auntie? She didn't come with you?"

Anna sniffed. "She's still annoyed by you being smart to her on the phone."

"I wasn't smart with her. I was calm. You know how that gets to her."

The women smiled at each other while Jordan studied them.

Amanda was long and lean, with an athlete's body. Her mother was short and round. And a redhead! She had the prettiest red hair Jordan had ever seen. But when they both smiled, the resemblance in their faces was uncanny. Jordan found himself wondering what Amanda's father looked like, and how much of those looks he had passed down to her.

Jordan smiled and ambled behind them into the house, almost forgotten by the women as they talked about all the things women talk about. Her mother oohed and aahed over the house, and when Amanda pointed out the handmade furniture, Anna turned to Jordan with a smile.

"You made that beautiful dresser?"

"Yes, ma'am."

She studied it with a critical eye. "You're very, very good."

Though Anna and Jordan were about the same age, her words of praise made him feel like a happy child. Perhaps it was Amanda's delight rubbing off on him. The feeling hadn't left when they sat down to a beautiful Thanksgiving dinner, all prepared by Amanda, another surprise from the woman who was proving herself to be full of them.

They held hands over the food, preparing for the blessing. Anna looked at Jordan and Amanda, at their joined hands, at the smile on her daughter's face, and her eyes softened with tears. "Things work out as they should, don't they?" she asked, her voice plaintive, quietly asking for forgiveness, even as she gave it.

"They do," Amanda agreed, not without a few tears of her own.

The women stared at each other for a moment. Jordan could feel the shift, the dropping of old hurts as they once again found common ground. He held both their hands, an unlikely connection between the women. The ease with which Anna had accepted him was still a bit startling. When she looked at him and smiled, he knew she approved of the relationship simply because Amanda was so happy. That really was all that mattered, and Jordan held enormous respect for that.

"Jordan, will you say grace?" Amanda asked.

He bowed his head, and paused a moment, gathering his thoughts, holding the hand of the woman he was already sure he could spend the rest of his life with. Even while the prayer formed on his lips, his one true thought ran circles in his head.

What a lucky man I am, to be in love with such a woman.

Chapter Eleven

Their idyllic bubble burst within an hour after Jordan returned to the Frost Building.

The Dean, Dr. Peter Barr, filled the doorway of Jordan's office. He was just as stern as he was broad, tolerating no breach of rules, no misuse of funds, no errors in scheduling. He ran the campus with a precision that had kept it ticking along like a well-oiled machine for his fourteen years on the letterhead.

He got away with being heavy-handed because he could also be surprisingly generous. Rumor had it that Dr. Barr was single-handedly responsible for keeping the benevolence fund overly healthy.

Today he seemed anything but generous as he stood in the doorway and boomed, "Dr. Eversole, we have a problem."

Jordan dropped his paperwork back to the desk and pulled his reading glasses from his nose. "Please come in and close the door, Peter."

Peter did as he was asked. He settled into a chair in front of Jordan's desk. He picked up a pen and started to fiddle with it while Jordan waited, knowing the Dean was forming his words carefully. He was a man who understood how one wrong word could burn bridges best left alone.

"I've received a few complaints, Jordan."

Jordan raised an eyebrow. "A few, or one in particular?"

Peter nodded. "A few from one person in particular, let's put it that way."

"How is my ex-wife doing these days?"

A brief smile flirted with Peter's lips. "After meeting her, I understand why she's your *ex*-wife."

Jordan sat back in his chair, waiting. These were just the pleasantries. He knew what was coming. He had dreamed about it for the last three nights, tossing and turning in bed while Amanda slept on beside him, seemingly without a care in the world. He envied her for being able to shut off the events of the day and fall into sleep so easily.

"You are familiar with a young woman named Amanda?"

Jordan nodded. He knew from watching the experiences of others at the college that being honest with Peter would be much better than the alternative. Peter hated liars, saw no excuse for them, and would make life a living hell for anyone who attempted to pull a fast one on him after they were caught doing something against policy.

"Amanda Whitmore," Peter clarified. "Is that right?"

"That's right."

Jordan was amazed at how calm he felt. His hands were steady, his breathing normal, his heartbeat fine. He had expected to be terrified at this point, but now that the time had come, he was ready for whatever the Dean would have to say.

"The complaint alleged a romantic relationship between you and Amanda," Peter went on. He looked at the closed door and then leaned forward, pinning Jordan with his dark eyes. "I understand a fling here and there, for God's sake, but a full-blown relationship? Jordan, what the hell are you thinking?"

Jordan swiveled his chair from side to side. How was he supposed to answer that?

Peter sat back and sighed. "It's true, then?"

"Yes. It's true."

Peter studied Jordan for a long while. "You know I can't let this happen here, don't you?"

The first tendrils of fear licked around the corners of Jordan's mind. "She's got three semesters left to go, then she's done. She already suggested transferring to another school, but she's on a really good track here. She could make the top five percent of her graduating class if she keeps her grades at this level."

"She's a good student, definitely. But that doesn't negate what we're discussing."

Jordan took a deep breath. "What exactly is going to happen here?"

"I didn't expect you to be so direct," Peter admitted. "You want to cut to the chase, then?"

"Please."

"Alright." Peter sat forward in the chair, his voice quiet. "You know the policy. It's in place for a reason, Jordan. If one student came forward and said Amanda was getting preferential treatment because she's dating a professor, the stain on the school wouldn't bleach out. Every student's grades would come into question. Your abilities as a teacher would come into question. My place as Dean would come into question, because it's my job, first and foremost, to make sure everything is above-board."

"I understand."

"The policy says a teacher will be terminated if a relationship with a student is ongoing. Notice that wording, Jordan. That's directly from the manual. Ongoing. That means there's still a way out of this, and there won't be any repercussions if you take that step right now."

Now Jordan's heart was racing. A blush of anger rose up his neck, coloring his cheeks. He knew the Dean was just doing what he had to do, but the mere suggestion of what he was being asked to do was enough to make him furious.

"You're saying I can have her or my job, but not both. You're saying I have to end it with her."

Peter shook his head sadly. "Jordan, this happens more often than you can imagine. Most professors have a little thing on the side now and again. You're surrounded by pretty, smart, ambitious women every single day, and it's inevitable that one or two will stand out and keep your attention. You might be a professor, but you're still a man, and you still have feelings. But you rarely hear about a teacher losing his position over a student because they are usually flings, Jordan. They come and go and every four years, a whole new crop is in the classroom. How do you know this woman is not one of those flings?"

"I'm in love with her."

Peter went slightly pale and leaned back in the chair. He looked as though he had just taken a sucker punch and still wasn't sure how he felt about the situation. "It's gone that far, then?"

"Yes."

"How does she feel?"

"She feels the same."

"And she knows ..."

"We've talked about what might happen if the board learned about our relationship, and regardless of those possibilities, my mind is made up."

Peter turned to look out the window. The leaves were all gone from the trees, the brilliant colors now little more than a carpet of brown on the quad. The bare branches rattled together when a strong wind blew. Peter watched them and contemplated Jordan's answer to the situation.

"You mentioned transferring."

"She has looked into it, but I'm not crazy about the idea. I don't want to interrupt her schooling. I don't want my job to make problems for her."

"Even if she does transfer, if the relationship continues, the board might look unfavorably on the issue."

Jordan rocked back in his chair. "Are you saying transferring won't matter?"

"Do you intend to marry her?" Peter asked bluntly.

"Would it matter?"

"No, I suppose not."

"So why all the questions? You know what you need to know."

Peter's voice rose on an exasperated exhale. "I'm trying to find a way around this, Jordan."

"Peter," Jordan said, his voice softening. "I know you are in a very bad position here. I'm sorry I put you there, and I appreciate that you want to find a way through this that will cause the least amount of hurt for everyone involved."

"Then you understand what I have to do," Peter said. "You're off until next Monday. Dr. Gleason will take over your classes. Get in that old truck and go home and think about things. Talk with Amanda if you feel you should. Make a decision and come back here on Monday to let me know what it is."

Though Jordan's heart sank, he knew the offer was much more generous than the Dean should have allowed. He recognized that Peter could get into trouble for giving him so much leeway, that his colleague was putting himself at risk to allow Jordan time to get his thoughts together.

"Thank you," he said, hoping his tone made clear how grateful he was. "That is really … That is above and beyond, Peter."

Peter stood up and studied Jordan for a moment. "Go home. Think things over. I know it's going to hurt either way, but at least it will be your choice, not something handed down by the board."

"Again … thank you."

"Jordan, there's one more thing." Peter looked directly at Jordan, making sure his point was clear. "Stains on an educator's record follow him forever. Word gets around. When a school hires someone new, they not only do the background checks, but they talk with former colleagues. If there are skeletons, they find them—and nobody likes to hire someone with bones rattling in their closet."

Jordan nodded slowly as Peter's words sank in. The situation was crystal clear. The Dean gave him a squeeze on the shoulder, wished him a good day, and closed the office door behind him when he left.

Jordan dropped his head to the desk and sat there, motionless, for many long minutes. He heard the bell announcing the start of class, but he knew there would already be a note on the door telling students to take the day off from that particular session. Peter was the kind of man who made all the necessary arrangements. Jordan would have to get the paperwork and class schedule to Dr. Gleason.

"What a mess," he murmured to the desk, refusing to raise his head. The wood was cool against his forehead. The phone rang and Jordan reached for it blindly, hit the button that would send everything to voice mail, and sighed at the papers underneath his nose. "What a mess."

He sent emails to Dr. Gleason detailing his class plans for the week. He finished grading the stack of papers in front of him, thankful it was one of his rare multiple-choice tests and not an essay assignment. He listened to another bell, gathered his things into his briefcase, and walked to the back doors of the Frost building. He did it all while in a daze, completely removed from the world around him.

In the parking lot, he climbed behind the wheel of the truck and looked out over the campus. Students went about their business. Some were walking on the sidewalks, in a hurry to get to class. A few were playing Frisbee, taking advantage of a day with unseasonably warm weather. On benches at the far side of the quad, a group sat with books open, studying together. Jordan watched as life moved on across the campus he loved.

Amanda's new car sat at the end of the parking lot. It was an older model, carefully selected for good gas mileage and repair history. She had received a settlement on her old car from the insurance company and could have purchased a nicer vehicle, but she preferred to save half the money and go with something less expensive.

She had also purchased a cell phone, something that she had avoided for a long while because of the high cost. She reasoned that if she was going to be driving out to his house, she might need it one day. "I might have a flat tire," she had said, and winked at him.

Jordan smiled as he remembered her considerations about the future, and he thought again of how mature she really was, how responsible.

She had warned him about this, hadn't she?

They had both known it was coming, but Jordan had been the one who kept his head in the sand, hoping the firestorm would blow over before it reached them. Amanda had been matter-of-fact about the whole thing, discussing nearby schools she could possibly attend, trying to engage him in a discussion on the inevitable. Jordan had changed the subject so often, it became a joke between them—but under that good-natured ribbing was a tension that said the storm was coming, just as surely as that hurricane had, and it was time to get ready for it.

Now that it was here, Jordan wasn't ready for it. He wasn't ready at all.

He considered calling Amanda on that new cell phone, letting her know about the week of forced vacation, but something in him kept his hand away from the cell phone. He knew she was in class, but that didn't matter—he could always leave a voice mail. What stopped him was much greater than the fear of inadvertently interrupting a classroom session.

Jordan started the truck and pulled out of the lot, trying hard not to look at Amanda's car. He remembered the way she had grinned when she pulled a spare out of the trunk, wrapped with a bright red ribbon, to replace the one she had borrowed from him many weeks before. Jordan had laughed out loud, the sound hard and deep, coming from somewhere inside that was entirely happy.

Now he wiped the tears from his eyes as he pulled onto the main highway.

When he got home, he marched straight to the bedroom, changed clothes, and popped open another can of paint. He started work again on one of the guest rooms, turning flat white walls into works of art with a brush and a sponge. He found that watching paint dry wasn't nearly as boring as the old saying went, but it gave him too much time to think.

While the second layer of paint was drying on the walls, he went back to work on the secretary desk downstairs, the same one he had started work on long before there was an Amanda and a relationship and the choice between the career he loved and the woman he adored. He carefully applied the brush, making his strokes perfect, spreading the paint with a sure hand. He paid attention to coloring within the lines.

Callie eased up beside him. She knew something was wrong with her man, and she could almost guess what. She missed the pretty girl who always cuddled her and said sweet things into her ear, and she knew Jordan missed her, too. Callie looked up at him with her best sorrowful pout, and she was rewarded with a short pat on the ears.

She meowed. Jordan looked down at her, his eyes wet.

"You aren't going anywhere. Are you, Callie?"

Callie meowed in answer.

"Love sucks," he said.

•

Amanda knew something was wrong. She knew it when she came down the sidewalk from the north side of the quad and saw Jordan's usual space in the parking lot empty. It was too early for lunch, and he had classes all day. She sped up, her feet moving faster while her heart pounded a tattoo of concern in her chest.

She stopped at the threshold of his classroom. It was empty. The handwriting on the board was foreign, definitely not Jordan's. She walked past his office—it was locked and empty, with no note on the door, no explanation offered.

Amanda stood looking at it, thinking. She pretended to scan the bulletin board when someone walked by, ignoring them while she contemplated what might have happened. Was he sick? She flipped open her new phone—one of the few splurges she had made lately—and dialed his number from memory, but the call went straight to voice mail.

Her next class began in less than five minutes. She kept reading the bulletin board as more students filed past, laughing and joking, some of them with their noses in their books, every other world going along just fine, while hers suddenly seemed off-kilter.

"You're overreacting," she whispered out loud, so as to hear the words and let them sink in. "You're making something out of what is sure to be nothing."

But as she sat in her classroom and didn't hear a word the teacher said, she knew her instincts were probably right. As soon as the bell rang, she ditched her next class and headed for her car.

•

Jordan heard the car long before it made it down to the house. The crunch of leaves and gravel under the tires made Callie shoot him a worried look, but soon she was purring and dancing around his feet, rubbing his legs in anticipation.

"Yeah, it's her," he said, filled with an absolute contradiction of happiness and dread.

Amanda parked beside Jordan's truck in the driveway. She stepped out of her car and looked at the house. The front door was open, and as she walked toward it, Callie streaked from behind the house and almost tripped Amanda in her rush of affection.

"Whoa, baby!" Amanda knelt and picked up the cat, who cuddled right against her chest and looked up at her with adoring eyes. "I remember a time when you didn't like me much."

Callie purred and stared into Amanda's face, perfectly content.

"Where's your daddy, huh?"

Amanda didn't knock on the door—they were far past the formal. She stepped into the house, noted the briefcase on the couch and the smell of paint. Jordan was sitting in the far corner of the dining room, putting the finishing touches on the huge desk he had been working on for as long as Amanda had known him. She was sure he heard her walk in, but he didn't turn around.

Amanda sat down in one of the dining room chairs. They had been refinished several weeks ago, and now they glistened with a high shine, a touch of elegance in the middle of what was still very much a construction zone. Callie settled on her lap with a loud purr, and together they watched the man they loved as he meticulously painted the massive piece in front of him. Not a word was exchanged while he finished his work, and then, finding no more to do, he turned to face her.

When she saw he had been crying, Amanda started to rise from the chair, but he held up a hand to stop her. "We need to talk, Amanda."

"Okay," she said, sinking back down to her seat. "Let's talk."

"The Dean came by my office today."

Amanda took a deep breath. She wasn't surprised by this development at all, especially since the outburst from his ex-wife on Thanksgiving morning—but she was surprised by his reaction to it. He looked as though he had just been told his best friend had died.

"We knew this was coming," she said as gently as she could.

Jordan sighed and ran his fingers through his hair. He left a small blue spot of paint near his temple. "But we never decided what to do about it. I guess that's why I was so stunned today. I knew it was coming, but it was an abstract. Like a hurricane out at sea—you look at it on the radar and it looks so far away, and so big, and you never think it could come for you."

Amanda nodded. "All we can do now is decide how to handle this, Jordan. The storm isn't here, you know? It's over.

Everybody knows. Now it's time to figure out how to put the pieces back together."

"I can't put them back." He wiped his eyes with the back of his hand, damning himself for crying all over again. He had done nothing but cry since he got home, and he wasn't that kind of man, was he? Surely he could figure this out and not be overcome by it. He was stronger than this.

"What did the Dean say?" she asked.

"He gave me an ultimatum," Jordan said. "He told me I can have my job, or I can have the woman I love, but I can't have both."

"That's not true," she said, startled that things had moved so quickly. Wasn't there a board that had to meet? Wasn't there some protocol for things like this? "I'm prepared to transfer somewhere else. I've already picked up the paperwork to make that happen. All I have to do it take it to the appropriate offices. There are only a few weeks left in this semester, and I can probably get in somewhere for the January start."

Jordan looked at her with blank eyes. "I brought that up with the Dean. He made it clear that transferring to another school would not set well with the board, and I would probably face dismissal regardless."

Amanda's mouth dropped open in surprise. "But they can't do that."

"Honey, they already did. It's been discussed. Dr. Barr was just the messenger."

Amanda held onto the sides of the chair. Callie jumped down, uncomfortable with the sudden tension in the room. She could taste the fear from both the humans, and she didn't want any part of it. She ran into the living room and curled up on the corner of the sofa, listening to their voices rise and fall.

"There has to be some sort of recourse," Amanda said. Her conviction was passionate, and she almost convinced Jordan with the mere determination in her eyes. "There has to be a set of checks and balances when it comes to the policy. If there weren't, anyone could be terminated for anything. What is the process to appeal something like this?"

Jordan shook his head, defeated. "Amanda, the policy is clear. It states that an ongoing relationship between a faculty and student is prohibited."

"But if I transfer ..."

"There are unwritten rules," he said softly. "Transferring at this point is just a gray area. It's not a solution. Even if they don't terminate me outright, they will find a reason. My performance evaluations will go down. Some of my grants won't be approved. Life will become difficult. It's the way the game is played."

"It's not fair," she hissed, tears springing to her eyes for the first time since their conversation began. "They can't do this to you."

"They have."

They stared at each other. The first shafts of true fear made their way into Amanda's heart. She spoke carefully, her words measured. "Have you made any decisions?"

Jordan sat forward in his chair and dropped his face into his hands. He breathed deep, the paint fumes making his head spin. "I'm going to take the rest of the year off. Next year, I'm going to find another job. I'm not sure where, just yet, or how I will be received by other schools, but all I can do is try, right?"

Amanda shook her head. "You can't do that."

"Then what do you expect me to do, Amanda? Break up with you?"

The words that had floated through her mind were now out in the open, and the sound of them frightened her more than anything else had in her life. "You love your job," she said, afraid to answer his question any other way.

He heard the fear in her voice and raised his head to look at her. "I'm turning in my resignation."

Amanda hadn't thought a heart could truly break, but she felt it then—the physical pain, right in the center of her chest, the terrible burning that made it hard to draw breath. Jordan had just made his commitment to her very clear, and that should have made her happier than any woman on earth. But to make that commitment, he had to give up something he loved just as much, something that had been a part of his life for much longer than she had, something that gave him immeasurable joy.

"You can't," she said again.

"Do you want to end this?"

Amanda flinched at the fury in his voice. She reached out

a hand to him, but she didn't move from her chair. She wasn't sure her legs would hold her. "No. No, Jordan, no. I love you."

"I love you, too, and that's why I'm doing this. Please understand, Amanda." Jordan rose from his chair and with three long strides he was in front of her, kneeling on the floor, taking her shaking hands in his calm ones. "I was so lonely. Then you came along and I wasn't lonely anymore, and I thought that was enough. I never dreamed I could fall in love again, but I did, and you became so much a part of my life that I started to forget you weren't there all along. I know that might not make any sense, but ... you fit into my life like you belong here, Amanda. I believe you do. If I have to make a choice that keeps you there, where you belong, then I'll do it."

"But you're a teacher," she wailed, the tears coming freely now. "This is not just what you do. It's what you love. I wish you could see yourself when you're explaining something in front of that class." She smiled and wiped her eyes. "You come alive, Jordan. You light up from the inside out."

"You do that to me," he murmured. "You do that same thing to me."

She wrapped her arms around his neck and held on tight. The sun was on its downward slope, peeking through the westward windows when the shakes finally stopped and the tears dried up. They moved through the house then, walking cautiously as if the very floor might fall out from under their feet, going through the motions of a normal evening.

Jordan made dinner while Amanda curled up on the couch. Jordan, believing they both deserved a little something, had opened a bottle of wine. She sipped from her glass while she stared at the television—the Weather Channel, appropriately enough—and thought about how love could be so beautiful, and laced with so much pain, all at the same time.

When they sat down to dinner, Jordan had calmed enough to discuss things rationally, but now Amanda seemed to be the one who was in another world. The look of shock in her eyes hadn't faded, even after he was sure all the tears would have washed it out. She ate very little and discussed everything but the elephant in the room, and then said it was probably time for her to go home. She had an 8:00 AM class.

The kiss she gave him at the door was fierce and possessive, the kind of kiss that begged to be finished in the bedroom. Before he could pull her back inside and take her there, she moved away with a final brush of her lips against his cheek, leaving him strangely sad and more than a little frustrated.

"I love you," she called from the car. Callie meowed from the porch. "I love you, too," she teased the cat, and Callie arched her back with pleasure.

As he watched her drive away, he wondered how long it would take before she accepted that he really did want to be with her enough to say goodbye to things that didn't matter nearly as much as she did.

He was in love with her. He was happier than he had ever been, and despite the heartbreaking decision he had been asked to make, he thought he had made the right choice. He could imagine life outside of the classroom, and the possibilities that might exist for a man who was a quick learner.

There were so many hobbies he could turn into full-time jobs, and besides that, a break from teaching in a classroom every day might do him some good. Maybe he could find a new, fresh way to teach, something that he hadn't considered before. The more he thought about it, the more he liked the opportunities that might be in store.

"We can do this, Callie," he said, suddenly filled with a sense of peace. "Everything happens as it should, doesn't it? Amanda taught me that. I think we can do this, and I think we might even be happier in the end."

The cat arched under his hand as he petted her, purring loudly. The night was cold, but Jordan stayed outside for a moment longer, breathing deeply of the air that heralded the approach of winter.

Jordan picked Callie up, opened the door, and went into the house to write his letter of resignation.

Chapter Twelve

Jordan drove into the campus the next morning. He was dressed in jeans and a polo shirt—definitely not appropriate attire for a professor at Sweetwater College—and he was singing at the top of his lungs to the radio as he drove into town. On the seat beside him was his briefcase, and in it were a few copies of letters, neatly folded in their envelopes, his final decision in writing.

He tried to call Amanda as he got closer to town, to wish her a good morning. He was sure she hadn't slept well, and he was worried about her. He got no answer.

When Jordan walked into Peter's office, the Dean smiled at the sight of him and boomed out a welcome. But when Jordan sat down in front of the desk and pulled out the letters, Peter's face went carefully blank.

"I've made my decisions," Jordan said.

"That was fast." Peter eyed Jordan suspiciously as he took the letter. He opened it and read the first line, then dropped it on his desk and rubbed his eyes. "This is a surprise."

Jordan shrugged. "I'm sorry that it came to this."

"I'm sorry, too."

"I wish I could stay. But I'm a big believer in following my heart, and my heart had its mind made up a long time ago. It just took time for the logical part of me to catch up."

"Amanda said something along those lines, too."

Jordan stared at Peter. "Amanda talked to you?"

Peter seemed just as surprised as Jordan was. "You didn't know?"

"Didn't know what?"

The truth of the situation suddenly dawned on Peter. He slowly pushed the letter back across the desk to Jordan and opened his desk drawer. "There's something you might want to see before you go through with handing those letters out, Dr. Eversole."

The Dean pulled a paper from his desk and slid it across the blotter. Jordan flipped it around with one finger. Amanda's name was at the top. In the space below it were red letters, making the situation crystal clear: *Withdrawn*.

"Oh, my God. No."

Jordan stared at the paper until it blurred. He wiped the tears from his eyes, surprised he had any left in him after yesterday's crying rampage. He studied every word of the withdrawal slip, memorizing the official end of Amanda's enrollment at Sweetwater College. No reason for the withdrawal was given, but he knew well enough what the reasons were.

Jordan looked at Peter, who shook his head sympathetically. "She beat you to the punch, my friend. She was here early this morning. I tried to talk her out of it, but once that young woman makes up her mind, she sticks with it."

"She never wavers," Jordan said, staring at the nightmare of words on the paper, now just a jumble in his head. "Can she be reinstated if I talk her out of this?"

"That's why it's in my desk instead of on its way to the Admin office."

Jordan stood up. "I've got to find her."

"You might want to take this," Peter said, holding up the letter of resignation.

Jordan snatched them out of his hand. "I'll be back with these," he said. "I'm resigning, and she's staying."

•

Jordan drove straight to her apartment, running a red light as he did so, getting the bird from a few irate drivers when he cut them off. He roared into the driveway of the apartment complex and banged on her door until the neighbor came out and gave him a dirty look. Her car wasn't in the parking lot.

"Amanda Whitmore—where is she?" he demanded.

"Are you her father?" the neighbor asked.

"No."

"Then I don't know where she is."

Jordan banged on the door again, this time more out of frustration than anything else, gave the neighbor the dirty look right back, and gunned his truck all the way out to the highway.

He drove around the campus, looking for her car. There was no sign of her. He went to the usual haunts and asked if anyone had seen her. No one had. He called her cell phone over and over, and got no answer. He left messages, trying not to sound frantic and failing miserably.

He went back home, hoping she would be there, somehow knowing she wouldn't be. He stormed into the house and rifled through the paperwork on the counter until he found the slip of paper with her mother's phone number on it. He contemplated the number, decided he was jumping the gun, and slid it into his pocket. He tried calling Amanda again, and this time, it went straight to voice mail.

She had turned her phone off.

Wait. Maybe it was just low on battery? Maybe she'd turned it off because she was in an office somewhere? Maybe …

Jordan sank to the sofa and buried his head in his hands. The shock of it all was starting to settle in, turning his limbs to heavy stones. He didn't have the strength to rise from the couch.

Amanda was gone.

He should have known last night, when she was so quiet after he announced his decision. He should have known by how hard she cried, and by the way she looked at him over dinner, as if she was dying inside but didn't know how to tell him. He should have known by the way she kissed him at the door before she left.

She had planned this. It wasn't a spur-of-the-moment decision. Amanda was not the kind to make such flighty choices. She had thought about it for a long time, even before the Dean came to Jordan's office and forced his hand. Amanda had set out a course for what she would do in any given situation, and when the time came, she had done it.

Calculating. Cold. How could he have missed it?

Jordan stalked back out to the car, slamming the door behind him so hard that it rattled in the hinges. He drove way over the speed limit all the way into town and went back to the apartment complex. This time he knocked on the manager's door.

"I'm looking for my girlfriend. Amanda Whitmore. Have you seen her today?"

The manager nodded. "Yes. She came in here early this morning and told me she had to move out. Something about a family matter?"

"And you just let her go? It's that easy?" Jordan was stunned by how quickly Amanda had made it all happen, how stealthily she had slipped from his reach.

The manager shrugged. "She was all paid up and her apartment looked just fine, so I told her I would send her security deposit. It's a college town, man. People come and go all the time."

"What address did she give you for the security deposit?"

The manager cast a wary eye at Jordan. "Who are you, again?"

"My name is Jordan Eversole. I'm a teacher at Sweetwater College."

"Thought you said you were her boyfriend?"

"I am."

The silence in the room was absolute. The manager stared at him for a moment, then opened the file in front of her. "She told me to send it in care of Anna Whitmore."

"That's her mother."

"Well, Mr. Eversole, that's all I know. I'm sorry I can't help you." The manager's demeanor was formal and clipped, and Jordan recognized the change for exactly what it was—a dismissal.

From there he went to the department store where she worked. The manager there couldn't give out any information, but she did make it clear that they were now hiring someone to take an open position—would any of his students be interested?

Jordan had to get out of the store before he said something he would regret.

As he drove through the campus again, he called Amanda's mother. Anna answered on the first ring. Before he could say anything more than her name, Anna started talking.

"She told me she was leaving, and then she did just that. I

don't know what the hell went on between the two of you, but she told me not to tell you anything, not that I know anything to tell you, anyway. She wouldn't tell me where she was going—her own mother, can you believe that? She keeps me in the dark on everything and I guess this is no exception."

"Anna, I can't find her. I'm looking everywhere."

Amanda's mother hissed at him in a voice filled with barely-controlled anger. "You leave her alone. I don't know what you did to my daughter, but by God, if you come near her again I will have your head. Understand?"

Anna hung up on him.

Jordan cursed and threw the phone at the dash. It bounced and landed on the floorboard. The little blue light mocked him for a moment before it winked out.

Just as quickly as it had come, his anger was spent. He pulled over on the side of the road and laid his head on the steering wheel. The desperation of the morning had finally drained him, making it impossible to see any way clear of what Amanda had done. Jordan watched the cars rush past and wondered when, exactly, he had missed the signs of what would come.

"Where are you?" he asked, but nobody was there to answer.

•

As Jordan was sitting on the side of the road and wishing he had done things differently, Amanda was crossing the state line. She had over a thousand miles to go, twice that much in her wallet, and all her possessions in the trunk. She was glad she had been thrifty, and saved for a rainy day, but she hadn't thought a rainy day like this one would ever come.

She wiped away the tears and held onto the wheel with both hands. The interstate spread out before her, and she darted between the slower trucks as she came through the Appalachian mountains. She knew staying in the same town with Jordan would be impossible, and she wouldn't be the one who ended his career. She couldn't live with herself if she allowed that to happen.

So she made the one decision she knew he would not make, and she had taken it out of his hands. He would be hurt for a while, and that hurt would turn to anger, and he wouldn't think kindly of her for a very long time, but eventually he would understand.

He would have done the same for her.

Amanda drove and thought about what love really meant, and how you knew when you were in it. She supposed it was the real thing when you cared enough about someone else to give up what you wanted for yourself, to let your life take a different trajectory than you had planned.

Maybe it was all about being selfless and giving the ultimate measure to someone else. Jordan had done it when he decided to resign, and now she had done the same for him by leaving him behind.

She pressed harder on the gas pedal. The tachometer shot up to seventy, and she came around a few coal trucks. The exhaust got into her lungs even though her windows were rolled up tight. She came up the mountain, the engine of her little car protesting, but making the climb just the same.

Had she covered all the bases? She had wanted to make certain Jordan couldn't find her. She had told the Dean this, and he had understood that, but he also reminded her that Jordan could access her files—if she transferred her grades somewhere else, he would be able to figure out where the paperwork had gone.

She decided then that she would wait until the end of the year to decide what to do, and go from there. She wouldn't give up her studies, but she did need the time to find a new job. The two grand in her wallet wouldn't last all that long, no matter how careful she was with the funds.

She had given her mother's home as a forwarding address, and had kept her phone turned off. She knew Jordan would call, and she knew he would leave messages, perhaps angry, perhaps pleading. She also knew she would stop at a hotel that night, lay in bed alone and listen to every one of them until the tears wore themselves out enough to let her fall asleep.

That's exactly what she did.

The next morning, Amanda woke with a throbbing headache. It was worse than a hangover. She looked at herself in the mirror and was shocked by how tired and gaunt she looked. She did the best she could with her makeup, and then forced herself to eat a good breakfast in the closest restaurant. The waitress looked at her with concern but said nothing, for which Amanda was grateful.

She called her mother to tell her she was alright. Anna was unusually subdued, and simply asked if Amanda needed anything. Anything at all? Amanda assured her she was fine, promised another phone call tomorrow, and hit the road.

It took her three days to make her destination. She could have made it in less time, but she wanted to take the back roads from time to time, to get away from the constant vigilance of the busy interstate and clear her head a bit. She cruised through small towns and contemplated where she would go, what she would do, and how long it would take before she could get her life back on track. She would. It was just a matter of time.

But it wasn't time yet. Safe and sound in the hotel on the outskirts of the city she would now call home, Amanda curled into a ball, wrapped her arms around her pillow, and cried herself to sleep.

•

Jordan got drunk.

He started with the bottle of wine he opened on the last night he had seen Amanda. When that was gone, he was still thinking of her, so he opened another bottle and drank some more. The next morning Callie watched as he stumbled to the bathroom, holding his head, swearing he would never touch another bottle of wine, no matter how many women broke his heart.

He spent the weekend lying on the couch, turning on the television just to ignore it, jumping when the phone rang and then getting upset all over again when he saw it wasn't Amanda calling.

His ex-wife, however, did call. He made it clear to Katie exactly how he felt, in terms that left absolutely no room for doubt. He yelled so loud, Callie had run under the table and turned to stare at him with wide eyes. When he was done, he threw the phone across the room and yelled some more. He felt better after that, but not nearly enough to make him get up off the couch.

On Monday morning he made himself get up, stumbled into the shower, did a terrible job of shaving and went to the Dean's office. He sat down in the chair uninvited, staring at Peter while the Dean stared right back.

"You look like hell," he announced, and Jordan uttered a bitter laugh.

"I should. I feel like it."

"You should take another week off."

"You don't want me to do that, Peter. Trust me."

Peter leaned forward and looked at him for a long moment. His phone rang, and he ignored it completely in favor of giving his full attention to the man in front of him. "What happened?"

"You know what happened. She left. End of story."

"Do you know where she went?"

"No. Do you?"

"I asked, and she refused to tell me."

Jordan smirked and looked at the window. "Figures."

Peter sat back in his chair. "Have you made a decision about your career here at Sweetwater?"

"I'm staying."

The Dean nodded and smiled. "Good. That's what I hoped I would hear from you. Are you prepared to start classes again today?"

"Starting with third period, yes."

"I'll call Dr. Gleason and let him know you need to meet with him this morning." Peter reached for the phone but didn't dial a number just yet. "Jordan, I want you to know …"

"I'm fine, Peter. I'll be fine."

"Maybe we should have a drink one night this week. Just catch up."

Jordan nodded, made no commitment to the offer, and left the Dean's office.

The campus looked like a different world to him as he walked to the Frost Building. The same students were on the same sidewalks and the same trees stood sentry over the same lawn, but Jordan felt removed from them, as though the world he had known was suddenly colored in different hues.

He went through the motions with Dr. Gleason, taking notes and trying to remember everything the younger man told him, knowing he would forget half of it as soon as he walked out the door. He stepped into his office and was surprised at the empty, stale smell of it, as though he had been away for many months instead of just a few days.

Classes resumed, and he did his best to catch up with where the students were. Something that should have been simple seemed difficult now.

He watched the students, saw their questioning eyes and heard their careless whispers, but for the first time, he didn't care what they thought. He was there to teach them and that was what he would do, and if they had speculation about his personal life, then they could just gossip all they wanted.

And gossip, they did.

"I heard he's sick. Something bad. Like cancer."

"I heard he's going to another school. Had a falling out with the Dean."

"My friend said he's finally gone crazy, rattling around in that old house with all those ghosts. That house is haunted, you know. Seriously."

The house *was* haunted—that much was true. Amanda's presence was everywhere. She had handled all his tools, helped with repairs and with building new furniture, had even worked on a quilt during those long, peaceful nights when they sat together on the couch and talked about nothing at all. Her lipstick was in the bathroom and her favorite food was in the fridge. Jordan couldn't bring himself to throw any of it out.

He went to work every day, and with the passing weeks it got easier. Then school ended for the semester, and when he would have been Christmas shopping for the woman he loved, he instead threw himself into working on the inside of the house, making sure it was ready for the winter winds that would howl off the ocean. At night he watched the news and wondered where Amanda was, and if she would ever let him know.

"Forget it," he said one night as he ate dinner with Callie. He had a tuna sandwich, and she was polishing off the rest of the can. "Forget her. She's not coming back. She doesn't give a damn about me or about you, kitty cat."

Man and cat looked at each other, both well aware he was lying.

Chapter Thirteen

Amanda liked her new job at the hospital. Though she was responsible for very little as a trainee, she was learning quickly, and the residents liked her. She enjoyed the feeling of being needed, or making someone smile when everything in their life was on the side of chaos. She went to work early and never hesitated to stay late. The staff admired her dedication and she quickly became a favorite among the nurses.

They knew something had gone wrong with her, something big, but no one was brave enough to ask what it was that made her stare off into space whenever she had idle time. She worked hard enough to drive away demons, and her co-workers simply assumed that was what she was trying to do, and left it at that.

She picked up brochures for the local university, and spent hours studying them, deciding what to do. All her credits would transfer, she was sure. She made a few calls to admissions and started pouring over the college course books as soon as they arrived in the mail.

She rented an apartment that was well below her means, scoured thrift stores for used furniture, and opened a savings account. She kept to herself and didn't give anyone an opening to get to know her better. She spent most of her nights at her apartment, reading books and trying not to think too much about the life she had left behind.

The upside of her decision was a renewed relationship with her mother. Amanda explained what she had done and why, and her mother was surprisingly sympathetic, doling out words of wisdom instead of advice. Amanda found this new side of her mother puzzling, but more than welcome.

Her mother called a week before Christmas to invite Amanda down to visit her. The invitation had been extended more than a few times, and each time Amanda had refused. Her reasons why were obvious: Jordan would probably come looking for her at her mother's house, and she knew she couldn't handle a confrontation with him. She would wind up falling into his arms and pleading forgiveness. Her conviction was strong, but she knew what her limits were.

Her mother sighed at the now-expected refusal, but then surprised Amanda with news. "I saw Jordan tonight."

Despite herself, hope leaped in her chest. "He came to your house?"

"No, no. I'm sure he's figured out where I live, but after I told him off over the phone, he wouldn't dare come here."

"Where was he?"

"At the restaurant downtown. What's the name of it? The one where you and your friends liked to go to get pasta?"

Amanda smiled, remembering. "Mario's."

"Mario's! That's right. He was there. Having dinner. I saw him through the front windows when I parked to go to the home interiors place next door. Buying a wreath for the door, you know—the old one is worn out. In fact, most of the Christmas decorations are worn out. It's amazing what a few years can do."

"How did he look?"

"He looked alright. His hair is longer now."

Anna stopped, and Amanda sensed what might come next, if she had the nerve to ask. Her mother went on about Christmas ornaments and lights, but the pause hung there between every sentence, pregnant with dread.

"Who was he with?" Amanda asked quietly.

Anna sighed. "Honey ..."

"It's alright, Mom. I'm the one who walked out of his life. He's free to do as he wants."

"I don't know who she was. She might have been his sister, for all I know."

A single tear ran down Amanda's face, but she kept her voice steady. "He's an only child."

"It was probably a colleague from work." Anna paused.

"Come to think of it, she looked like a teacher."

Amanda smiled at the way her mother tried to make things better than they really were. "It's okay, Mom. I'm glad to know he's getting back on his feet. I'm happy for him."

Anna chuckled wryly. "Sweetheart?"

"Yeah?"

"Moms always know when their daughters are lying."

•

Jordan had been out on a date. He had taken out one of Peter's friends, a woman who worked at the local bank. She was beautiful, tall and willowy, with blonde hair that almost touched her waist. She laughed at his jokes, discussed current events with a passionate opinion, and engaged him entirely for the space of two hours. But as soon as he rose to pay the bill, his thoughts turned to Amanda—and suddenly, he didn't want to be anywhere but at home. Alone.

Life was like that lately. He might find something or someone to keep him busy for a few hours, but suddenly his reality would intrude, and the void left by Amanda's leaving would swallow him up again. He hoped the small steps back into the normal world—dating, for instance—would help him move on. More often than not, he suspected those forays into distraction were doing him more harm than good.

He dropped the beautiful blonde at her door with a gentle kiss on the cheek. He could feel her puzzled eyes on him as he walked back to his car. Everything had gone incredibly well between them, there had been real chemistry there, but he had shut her down cold at the end, and she was probably wondering what the hell his problem was. He didn't blame her. If the situation had been reversed, he would have been annoyed, too.

Callie met him at the door. He scooped her up and wandered around the house, aimlessly looking at things he had seen a thousand times before. The house was neat as a pin, everything in its place, an order that Jordan had never really cared about before, but insisted upon now. It was like a little ocean of control in a world where he felt he had none left.

He considered calling her mother again. He had the number memorized by now. He had dialed six numbers more often than he would like to admit, and then had lost his nerve before he could dial that seventh digit. He wasn't sure why he was afraid. The thought of finding Amanda was something he dreamed about, but the thought of Amanda rejecting him one final time was enough to make him wary of finding her at all.

Tonight he looked at the phone, contemplating it. Christmas was a week away. School was out for the holiday. Somewhere, Amanda was probably decorating an apartment, maybe wrapping presents for her mother. Her mother would have to know where she was by now, wouldn't she?

What did he have to lose?

At the sixth digit, Jordan lost his nerve. He didn't think he could handle Anna's anger, especially with the knowledge that she knew where Amanda was, and she would probably refuse to tell him. Getting that close to her would be almost like seeing her though a crystal-clear window, but not being able to reach her through a sheet of glass.

He tossed the phone onto the couch and laid back, closed his eyes, and once again started the nightly battle of clearing his mind so he could sleep. The cat jumped up on the couch, sniffed at the phone, and cast a worried look at her man.

Callie watched him until the hour became late, and when he finally started to breathe deep and quiet, she curled up beside him, protecting him as best she could.

•

In the morning Jordan woke with an aching back and a throbbing headache. He immediately stubbed his toe on the coffee table and hollered words that would make him cringe, had he been in any mood to care. His bad mood got even worse when he spilled orange juice all over the counter as he made breakfast. He finally climbed into the shower and stood there, sure that it might be the only safe place in the house.

He went into town that afternoon to shop for essentials. He needed basic staples, as he was loudly reminded that morning. Callie was out of tuna and howled every time he walked past the kitchen.

The colors of Christmas didn't strike any cheer for Jordan this year. He hadn't even hung a wreath. He watched as women searched through garland and ornaments, trying to find the perfect fit for their homes. He was turning the corner when he caught sight of something that stopped him cold.

It was a woman. A small, thin woman with shoulder-length brunette hair. Jordan watched as the overhead lights danced along the blond strands scattered throughout the darker sea. She had a spring to her step, humming quietly along with the piped-in music, and she was wearing a red sweater that looked like one he had seen Amanda in so often …

"Amanda?"

The name was a whisper—his voice suddenly didn't work. Jordan left his buggy in the middle of the aisle and rushed over to the other side, his eyes glued to the woman who had yet to turn around and see him. Pure joy ran through him as he touched her on the shoulder, wanting to wrap his arms around her already, not sure of what to say, scared to death and happier than ever, all at the same time.

The woman turned around and looked up at him with green eyes. Jordan let his hand fall away, the breath knocked out of him.

It wasn't Amanda.

"Can I help you?" the woman asked, and Jordan shook his head, backing away. He mumbled an apology and headed straight for the door, his way blurred by tears. When he got out into the fresh air, he breathed as deeply as he could, letting the coldness sear his lungs and hurt his chest. He stumbled to the car and sat there for a long time, his mind blank, his heart broken all over again.

That's when he made the decision his heart knew was right all along.

He drove home at a breakneck pace, not caring if he was pulled over or not. Once there, he yanked the resignation letters out of the big secretary desk. He hadn't been able to throw them away, and he wasn't sure why—but now he knew.

The next stop was the college, where he rang the Dean's office. Though school was out for the students, some members of the faculty used the time to catch up on work and prepare for the new semester. Jordan had known the Dean long enough to know where he would find him. When Peter opened the door, his face was etched with worry.

"Jordan? Are you alright?"

Jordan smiled. It felt foreign to have a real smile on his face, one that wasn't hiding the pain within. He handed the letters to a shocked Peter. "Not yet, but soon, I'm going to be much better."

Peter rifled through the letters and then looked up, his eyes bright. "These are …"

"Yes."

Much to Jordan's surprise, Peter smiled. "Good for you, Jordan. Good for you."

"Thank you for the time to make the right choice."

Peter waved the comment away. "Do you know where she is?"

"No. But I'm going to find out."

Peter clapped Jordan on the shoulder, then let go of the formalities and pulled him into a hug. The two men embraced while Peter said, "If you need a recommendation for any other school, any other position, I'll give you the best one they've ever seen."

Jordan nodded and said his goodbyes, grateful for the colleague who had become his friend. He went back to the car, where he closed the door and opened his phone, dialing the number by heart. This time, he didn't hesitate to dial the last digit.

Anna answered on the first ring.

"It's Jordan."

The silence stretched out, long and hard, and Jordan thought for a moment she had hung up on him. Then she sighed, and it was a sound filled with relief.

"I want to apologize," Anna said. "I'm sorry for the way I treated you the day Amanda left. I understand now, I know it wasn't your fault, and I should never have blamed you."

"I was terrified you would be furious with me. That's why I didn't call."

"I didn't call you because I didn't know what to say."

Jordan chuckled. "As Amanda once said, we need to work on our communication."

Anna chuckled with him, then sighed again. "I'm really sorry, Jordan."

Jordan closed his eyes and swallowed hard. "Thank you. All

is understood and forgiven, Anna."

"I guess you want to know where she is."

Jordan laid his head against the back of the seat. "I saw a woman in the store today. She was the same size as Amanda, same hair color, same everything. She was even humming along with the radio, and you know how Amanda does that? Always hums along without realizing she's doing it?"

Anna laughed.

"I went up to this woman and I thought it was her, Anna. But then she turned around and it wasn't, and after all this time, it was like losing her all over again."

"I'm sorry," Anna said. Jordan could hear the pain in her voice. "I'm so sorry."

"Tell me where she is."

Anna was quiet for a long moment. "She did it for you, Jordan. If you go looking for her, it's going to tear her apart all over again. You'll be in the same boat you were in before she left. Tell me, Jordan—is that fair to anyone? Especially my daughter?"

"I just resigned my position, Anna. Whether I have Amanda back or not, I'm gone."

A laugh gurgled from the other end of the line. "Well, why didn't you say so?"

The sudden shift in attitude shocked Jordan into a smile. That moment would forevermore be a snapshot in his memory, that moment when he felt true hope for the first time in what seemed like a lifetime.

"Where is she?"

"You know," Anna said pensively, "if I tell you outright, she's going to blame me for it, and if things don't work out the way you hope they will, she's going to stop talking to me again. I don't want to go through that. Let me think of a way around this."

Jordan did laugh then. She was going to tell him!

"Amanda always did have a place she went when she was feeling lost. It was the place where she felt closest to her father. She grew up in his planes, did you know that? He was a pilot. He took her up all the time, no matter how worried I was about plane crashes. He said it was safer than taking her anywhere in the car. After he was gone, when she needed to be close to him, or to figure something out, she would drive out to the airport and watch the planes take off. It gave her a lot of peace to be where her father loved."

The memory of Amanda's file flashed through his head. He had stared at it for hours after she left, memorized every little piece of information, as if that would somehow bring her back. The whole time, he had been staring at the answer.

"Anna, thank you."

"You're welcome, and you better go. I think you have a plane to catch."

Jordan said goodbye, hung up, and dialed again. This time directory assistance put him through to the airport, where he was connected with the ticket counter.

"I need a one-way ticket to Chicago," he said.

Chapter Fourteen

The snow was falling. It hadn't stopped all day, and now the sidewalks were covered with four inches of the white blanket. Amanda pulled the quilt tighter around her shoulders and sipped her hot cocoa. She had made a special trip to the store just to get some when she saw the forecast. The first snowfall of the year was not complete without a steaming mug of chocolate.

Outside her fourth-floor window, the streetlights shone down on the busy traffic, moving along at a good clip despite the slippery conditions. From her stereo, Christmas music was playing. She watched the city roll by while her mind went to South Carolina, where her mother was planning on spending Christmas with Auntie.

There would always be good food on the table and more than a few presents under the tree. Some of them would be addressed to her. She glanced back at the package on the table, the one filled with presents she would send home tomorrow.

She loved Christmas, loved shopping for the perfect gifts, but this year had been melancholy. She had considered getting a kitten to take the edge from the loneliness, but she still wasn't entirely sure where she would land. Her job was a good one and she enjoyed it, but she had to focus on starting her schooling again. She wouldn't let too much time pass before she went back and finished up her degree.

She wondered where Jordan was, and how things were going with the house, and whether Callie missed her. She wondered, more often than she should have, if he had gone out with that woman again, and if he was moving on. Was he getting over her?

She wasn't getting over him, that was for sure. She still dreamed about him at night, and sometimes thought she heard his voice. She searched for him among strangers, thought about him whenever she saw a piece of handmade furniture, and longed so many times to pick up the phone and call. His desperate phone calls had ended soon after she left, and though she should have been grateful, she was anything but.

A cab stopped in front of the building. Brake lights flashed. Horns honked as a car slid on the ice, almost careening into the nearest pole before straightening out. A man stepped from the cab, looked down at a paper in his hand, and looked up at the door. He headed for it with purposeful strides.

Amanda shook her head to clear it. For a moment she had thought of Jordan, the way he walked, the way his hair was pushed back by the breeze ... but that was wishful thinking. He had no idea where she was.

The knock on the door made her jump.

It was a quiet knock, but entirely unexpected. Someone had obviously lost their way. Amanda made sure the chain was in place—a woman could never be too careful, especially in the busy city—and opened the door just a crack. "Can I help you?" she asked.

There was no answer. The visitor shifted, their feet making stamping sounds on the old, worn carpeting in the hallway. Amanda started to close the door when the voice came.

"Amanda?"

That voice, the one she had thought she would never hear again, surprised her so much that she backed away from the door. She stared at the small opening, unable to see anything through it. Surely she had heard what she wanted to hear, not what was really there. She missed him so much, she was now creating him out of thin air, wasn't she?

I need to see a shrink, she thought.

"Amanda, it's me."

That voice was unmistakable. Amanda moved slowly, the disbelief turning her limbs wooden. She pushed the door closed, undid the chain, and swung open the door.

Jordan stood in the hallway, wrapped up in a long coat, snowflakes trapped in his hair. His eyes were suspiciously bright, his smile cautious.

"May I come in?"

Dozens of questions ran through her head all at once. *How did you find me? How did you get here? Why did you come? What do you want? Do you have any idea how leaving you broke my heart? Do you know how happy I am to see you?*

The questions crowded out every other thought until there was no room for words. She opened her arms and he stepped into the room, sweeping her up in a bear hug so tight, she could hardly breathe. She clung to him, her fingers in his hair, as he pressed his lips to hers.

•

The joy that ran through Jordan was unparalleled. There was no doubt in his mind—or his heart—that he had done the right thing this time. He was exactly where he needed to be, with this beautiful woman who had stolen every part of him for herself, and he couldn't imagine being anywhere else. He couldn't wait to tell her.

With great effort, Jordan released her and pushed her gently away from him. He looked into her eyes while he said what he had to say. "I understand why you left. I respect your reasons, no matter how much it hurt. But I want you to know that when I said my mind was made up, it was. I resigned this morning, Amanda. I'm no longer a teacher at Sweetwater College."

She took a step back, startled that he would make such a move. Didn't he know she had given up everything so he could keep the job he was born to do? "Jordan, you can't."

"I have. It's over. If you won't have me, that's something I will have to live with—but my mind is made up. What I want, more than anything else, is to be with you."

"But I did this!" she yelled, raising her voice and shocking Jordan into motionlessness. "I left you, and it was the hardest thing I've ever done, or will ever do, and you—you … How could you?"

Jordan opened his mouth to speak but had no idea what to say.

"I did the right thing, and now you've thrown it all away. Don't you understand? You'll never get another teaching job! All those things that made you so happy, you'll never have them again. I wanted you to have them. I wanted you to be happy."

Jordan shook his head. "No! Amanda, those things don't make me happy if I don't have you. Don't you understand? It's all about you, it has been from the night that hurricane came through, and it always will be. That's why I'm here. I love you, and I'm not letting you go without a damn good fight."

The tears finally broke free. Huge, racking sobs gripped Amanda, doubling her over, making it almost impossible to breathe. Jordan gently led her to the couch, where fought to get control. All the emotion of the last month apart finally bubbled to the surface, and it was enough to almost make her sick. She bent her head low and took deep breaths to calm down.

When she looked up at him again, he gave her the faintest smile. "It's been bad," he said.

"I'm sorry," she said.

"I understand why you did it," he said. "So you don't have to apologize ever again."

"You really resigned?"

"I really did. Without you, there wasn't any joy in what I was doing. There wasn't any point in being there. Believe me, handing over that resignation letter was the best I've felt in weeks."

Amanda cuddled close to him, still hardly believing he was there, in her apartment, half a world away from where they had begun.

"My mother told you, didn't she?"

"No."

"How did you find me?"

Jordan paused, thinking of a way to answer. Finally he shrugged and said, "Your father."

Amanda smiled at that.

"I wish he were here. He would have loved you."

Jordan laughed. "He would have chased me out of town with a shotgun of stealing his little girl."

"Well, there is that."

They sat together quietly on the couch, giving their hearts time to heal, steeping themselves in the reality of each other after many long weeks of being apart. Finally Amanda looked up at him and smiled.

"How long are you going to stay?"

Jordan shrugged. "I dropped Callie off with your mother and came straight here—"

"My mother!"

"Yeah. Callie took to her like she was her best friend."

"She broke out a can of tuna, didn't she?"

"She was spooning it into the dish when we got there."

Amanda laughed.

"I told the airline I wanted a one-way ticket, and that's what I got. So I'm here until you don't want me here anymore, I guess." Jordan eyed her closely. "Do you want me here?"

"Yes! Of course I want you here."

"Good. Because I don't think I can get another cab on a night like this, and it's too cold to sleep on your doorstep."

She playfully punched him in the arm. He caught her hand and kissed it.

"Let's take it day by day," he suggested. "We can make decisions soon, but right now we don't have to worry about anything but each other."

Amanda stood up from the couch and held her hand out to the man she loved. "Then let's start worrying about each other. Come to bed with me, Dr. Eversole."

Jordan smiled, took her hand, and followed her to the bedroom.

•

On Christmas morning, Anna was putting the final touches on her special holiday ham. She drizzled a bit more brown sugar over the top, pushed it back in the oven, and looked over at Callie. The cat was sitting in the middle of the kitchen table, watching every move with intent.

Anna reached back into the oven, gingerly pulled a small piece of ham, and blew on it to cool it down. When she presented it to Callie, the cat purred with happiness. Everything the animal did seemed to endear her a little more, and Anna was starting to dread the moment Jordan would come back for her.

"I could get used to you," Anna told her, rubbing her arched back.

When the doorbell rang, Anna hurried to answer, casting a worried look back at her kitchen. "Now, you know I don't have that dinner ready yet, Marilyn! It won't be on the table until noon sharp ..."

Her voice disappeared at the sight on her doorstep.

Jordan stood with arms full of gaily wrapped presents. His hair was tousled by the wind, his hands wrapped in fine leather gloves. Beside him stood Amanda, bundled up in a thick coat, her nose red from the wind. Their matching smiles were enormous.

"Merry Christmas," Amanda chimed, and Anna wrapped her grown-up little girl in her arms. Jordan stepped into the house and carefully placed the gifts under the tree, then greeted Anna with a warm hug.

"Thank you," he whispered into her ear.

She sniffled.

"You found her!"

"What's for dinner?" Amanda asked, already dipping into the platter of cornbread dressing. When Anna shooed her away from it, she picked up a thumbprint cookie filled with grape jelly and ambled over to the table to give Callie a kiss. The cat purred as she was passed around between the three humans she adored most, listening while they talked about snow in Chicago, hurricanes in August and Christmas with Aunt Marilyn, who was sure to have a thing or two to say about all this.

Marilyn didn't have much to say at all, as it turned out. She took one look at Jordan, declared him the most handsome man she had seen since her late husband, clapped her hands together and said, "Let's eat!"

Minutes later, the four of them sat around the dinner table. Anna poured wine while Jordan sliced the ham. Jordan said grace, the words so much more potent than they were over the Thanksgiving table, because now they knew what it meant to live without one another.

Anna caught the way Jordan and Amanda gazed at each other over the table, and her heart caught in her throat. It was so very much like the look of love she had given her husband, many years ago.

The opening of the gifts was a festive affair. Callie was right in the middle of it, having a fine time of chasing bows and ripping the paper. For Anna there was a sweater with a matching scarf, a few bottles of luxurious bubble bath, and a few CDs to listen to while she soaked. For Marilyn there were cookbooks, a bottle of fine Italian wine and a framed picture of the ocean. Jordan opened his gifts with undisguised glee—a book on advanced woodworking, a new pair of carpenter's gloves, and a lovely antique vase for his home.

Even Callie got in on the act, receiving a new silver dish and a pillow filled with catnip, which she tossed merrily about, meowing with pleasure.

Amanda, being the darling of them all, was showered with presents. She was studying a new book on archeology when Jordan stood up in front of her and said, "There's one more present for you."

She looked at the tree and back up at him, waiting.

"I know we haven't known each other long," he said. "But we've come to know each other in a way that some people never do, even after a lifetime of being together. I think our love is sweeter now, because we know what it feels like to lose each other. The thought of going through that again ..." Jordan paused, thought for a moment and shook his head. "The thought of that frightens me more than I can say."

Amanda nodded and took his hand.

"But maybe it was a blessing. Because it made me realize how much I really do want you in my life, and how much I have loved you from the start. I can't imagine being with anyone other than you. And I think that's why this is the most appropriate gift I can give you."

Jordan held out his other hand, and Amanda gasped.

The ring sparkled with the glow of the Christmas lights. It was beautiful, understated, and the perfect size for her hand. It was just the kind of ring Amanda would have hoped to have if she ever got married, but she had never hoped for such a surprise so soon. Now that it was here, she realized she was more than ready for the next step. She wanted to be with Jordan for the rest of her life.

"I know this is sudden," he went on. "I know this is the last thing you expected, that we haven't even discussed it yet—but I know that even if you tell me no right now, I will keep waiting, and asking, and even begging if I have to, until you say yes. My life isn't complete without you in it."

Amanda nodded and tried to speak, but the tears were too much.

"I want to grow old with you. I want to take care of you when you're sick and share the good times and have dozens of babies and sit on the front porch in our rocking chairs while the rest of the world turns on without us. Amanda ..."

She was laughing and crying when he knelt down in front of her with a smile, and before he could even ask the question, she threw her arms around his neck.

"Yes!"

Jordan threw her arms around her and pulled her close. Anna laughed and cried all at the same time. Marilyn clapped her hands in celebration and laughed out loud. Even Callie got in the act, pushing her head between Amanda and Jordan, meowing at the melee and sniffing at the ring as Jordan slipped it onto Amanda's finger.

Sure enough, it was a perfect fit.

Amanda was sure that for as long as she lived, she would never forget that moment. The best part of it, and the first thing she would always recall when her mind went back to that magical Christmas, was the way her engagement to the man of her dreams was ushered into the world—on the wings of happy tears and beautiful laughter.

Epilogue

Five years later...

The summer wind blew through the trees as Jordan pulled into the drive. The big house in the middle of nowhere was surrounded by late-season flowers, a cacophony of color that drew songbirds and butterflies. A rope swing hung from the tallest tree in the yard, the seat already worn by hours of happy use. On the porch were two rocking chairs, moving slowly with the breeze.

He climbed the steps, opened the door, and was greeted by a meowing Callie. He scratched her ears and walked into the kitchen, where he found a warm spice cake on the counter, covered with a dish towel. Unable to resist, he reached in and pulled off a little piece. The scent was heavenly, and the taste was even better.

He set his briefcase on the secretary desk. Now the paint was slightly worn from use, and in the cubbyholes were rolled pieces of paper, crayon masterpieces that made Jordan smile every time he looked at them. Standing there in the quiet house, he noticed a new one and pulled it out for inspection.

It was a blue background and a bright white swirl in the middle of it. He studied it for a moment, unsure of what it was, then suddenly it dawned on him. He grinned and rolled it up, stuck it in one of the few cubbies that were empty, and shook his head.

They really watched too much of the Weather Channel.

He snuck another pinch of the spice cake into his mouth and stuck his head out the back door, hollering, "Amanda, honey?"

She was there behind the house, holding the hand of a little boy who looked just like his father. The boy was pointing to something in the grass with one chubby finger, gabbing in baby-speak to his mother. Jordan gazed at his wife and their son, watched the boy's hair glisten in the afternoon sunlight, and again gave silent thanks that all those years ago, he had made the right decision.

The boy came toward him, his little legs just now steady enough to let him run, and Jordan swung him up onto his hip. He gave Roman a kiss and got a hug in return. "Lookie, Daddy!"

The butterfly was huge, his wings spread flat as he rested on a flower in the backyard. Father and son studied it for as long as it let them, and then they watched as it flew away and became a speck in the distant sky.

Amanda watched them, content to simply observe as they played together. She had thought she couldn't love anyone more than Jordan, but the moment she heard Roman cry in the delivery room, she knew she was wrong. Her whole world was suddenly washed in a new spectrum of colors, a palette she had never imagined could exist. The force of it was impossible to deny. She watched as Jordan cut the cord, then cried happy tears as her husband held their newborn son. The look of pride and love on his face mirrored the very emotions coursing through her.

If the love for her husband was beyond all comprehension, then what was this?

A miracle, she decided. *This must be what a miracle feels like.*

That miracle had been a long time in coming. The first year of their marriage was a constant struggle to stay afloat as even the most basic bills ate them alive. Amanda went back to school and took a heavy load, trying to finish as soon as possible.

Jordan worked as a carpentry apprentice—his "learning vacation," as he so often put it—and the pay wasn't good enough to keep them afloat. They came dangerously close to losing the house, and that was hard for both of them to take. They both took odd jobs, and managed to scrape by. Neither of them ever complained, because they knew things would be easier in the long run—if only the short run didn't kill them first.

The day Amanda graduated was a huge celebration, and she moved into a position right away, taking an administration job with the local hospital. The pay was good, the colleagues were friendly, and Amanda settled in nicely, even earning two raises that first year. The finances began to ease, and they started to see the light at the end of the tunnel.

Jordan had trouble finding a job—even with the Dean's good recommendation and glowing testimony from his former colleagues at Sweetwater College, the potential schools looked askance at him as soon as they realized how young his wife was, that she was barely out of college herself. It was discrimination, plain and simple, but there was no law against the kind they were facing. There was nothing they could do but keep trying and hope that someone eventually gave Jordan a chance to prove what a good teacher he really was.

There were nights when Jordan would walk the floor in frustration, and Amanda would reassure him over and over, silently praying that her words of encouragement would be proven right in the end.

When he finally did get a job on a trial basis, he impressed the staff so much that he was asked to stay on. He worked hard, completely dedicated to the students, and he slowly became more content than Amanda had ever seen him. A mere three years later, he became Principal of Sweetwater High School.

Shortly after that, she became pregnant with Roman. When she gave Jordan the news, he reacted with instant happiness. Their world finally felt complete.

Now Amanda slipped up behind her husband and wrapped her arms around him. Her body had been fuller since his birth, more voluptuous and lovely, if such a thing were even possible. Jordan was Jordan turned his head for a kiss and Amanda obliged, taking her time, enjoying him just as much as she always did.

"This is paradise, isn't it?" she murmured, and he smiled against her lips.

"It's better than paradise."

The weather was calm, but they knew a storm was coming. The swirl of white on the picture Roman had drawn had been inspired by what he saw on the television lately. A massive hurricane was headed their way, and though it was expected to spare the town of Sweetwater this time, everyone was being very cautious. Jordan knew that this time, they would evacuate before the storm hit. There was much more at stake now.

He watched their son toddle around the yard and smiled. Callie, entirely happy with the way things were shaping up these past few years, followed Roman around, ready to pounce at whatever the boy might find interesting. Amanda and Jordan watched as Roman bent low and carefully patted the top of Callie's head.

"How is the storm looking?" he asked Amanda.

"About one hundred miles off the coast right now, but it's going to start showing any minute. This is a big one."

They watched the white clouds move casually across the sky, trying to trick them into thinking Mother Nature was entirely benign.

"Should we leave? Go visit your Momma for a while?"

"Not just yet. They haven't canceled schools yet, have they?"

"Not yet. They will tomorrow, I'm sure." He kissed her temple. "We can probably go ahead and make plane reservations tonight."

Anna had surprised them both the year before when she announced that she was moving back to Chicago. She missed her old home, she said, her old city, the pulse of life that flowed through it day and night. She longed for the winter snows and the icy wind and the hot, hot summers. She even missed the sound of planes flying over, she said, and so it was fitting that her new home was under a flight path out of O'Hare.

When they visited her—which was quite often—Roman slept peacefully under the regular schedule of roaring jets overhead. Anna often commented on how much Roman looked like Jordan, but how much he acted like Amanda.

Amanda looked at her husband now and felt that same swelling of love, followed by the overwhelming gratitude, thanks for the joy they had found in each other. She loved seeing their love grow, and she knew it was going to get even bigger as the years went on.

She whispered in his ear, "I was wondering something."

"Do tell."

"Remember when we first got married, that very first night together as husband and wife?"

He grinned. "How could a man ever forget such a thing?"

"Remember when you said you wanted to have a dozen babies with me?"

Their son wandered through the backyard in pursuit of some small winged creature. Jordan turned and took her into his arms. "I do remember."

"Did you really mean that?"

He laughed and kissed her nose. "Absolutely."

Amanda gave him a smile he had seen before, the one that said she had a secret, and a delightful one at that. The changes in her body over the last few weeks suddenly made sense. His heart started to pound as his wife smiled into his eyes.

"Good," she said.

•••

Shannon Dauphin

Shannon Dauphin is a writer who has been in the publishing industry in one form or another for more than a decade. When she's not writing, she loves to cook, explore antique stores and travel. She and her husband reside with their children in an historic home near Nashville, TN.

A stunning older woman. A mysterious younger man. A garden of infinite possibilities. When Lily McVay needs help keeping the terms of a rather unorthodox divorce settlement, the bond between her and handsome Will may prove that more is blooming than just the flowers.

www.ingramcontent.com/pod-product-compliance
Lightning Source LLC
La Vergne TN
LVHW090958080826
845145LV00003B/1043

* 9 7 8 1 9 3 4 9 1 2 0 1 0 *